GRINNY

Also by Nicholas Fisk

Science fiction and fantasy
  High Way Home
  Little Green Spaceman
  Space Hostages
  Trillions

Other titles
  The Bouncers
  Lindbergh the Lone Flier
  Making Music
  Richthofen the Red Baron

GRINNY

A Novel of Science Fiction

by

Nicholas Fisk

publishers since 1798

THOMAS NELSON INC.

NASHVILLE / NEW YORK

Copyright © 1973, 1974 by Nicholas Fisk

All rights reserved under International and Pan-American Conventions. Published by Thomas Nelson Inc., Nashville, Tennessee. Manufactured in the United States of America.
First U.S. edition

Library of Congress Cataloging in Publication Data

Fisk, Nicholas.
  Grinny; a novel of science fiction.

  SUMMARY: Eleven-year-old Tim records the strange events that occur during Great Aunt Emma's visit and his growing conviction about her true identity.
  [1. Science fiction] I. Title.
PZ7.F548Gr   [Fic]   74–10274
ISBN 0–8407–6409–X

GRINNY

Timothy Carpenter's
Introduction

I was only eleven when Great-Aunt Emma came to stay with us. My sister Beth was nine and my friend Mac (real name Steven) Rainier was eleven too. Now I am fifteen. I was too young to have done anything about Aunt Emma when she was with us because I was never sure what it all meant, and even when everything got frightening and sinister I could neither have proved anything nor gone to someone for help.

This book is based on my diary and other writings of the Aunt Emma period. My diary was a Christmas present, a big bound book in blue Morocco leather with gold-edged leaves. I remember how excited and pleased I was when I first started writing in it and thinking how handy it was that Aunt Emma had come just at the right time, to give me something exciting to write about.

And then, later on, it all turned sour, and I used to be almost frightened of the diary and of writing the next page. Everything I had written seemed to add up to something horrible. The more I wrote, the more certain it seemed that the horror was true and would get worse. I do not keep a diary anymore.

I showed the diary to Mr. Nicholas Fisk, the writer, as a result of talking to him about my wanting to be a reporter. Of course, I can never talk to my father and mother about Aunt Emma—they quite literally *would not hear me*. You will understand why when you have read this book.

Mr. Fisk said that I should get the Aunt Emma story published if I want to make people aware of the possibilities facing them and to prepare them for the next time —if there is a next time. It is Mr. Fisk's opinion that the danger is most probably over—the thing happened, the experiment failed and there would be no point in trying it again.

I wish I could feel sure he is right.

Diary

BOOK ONE

January 14

Astonishing news! I had come back from Mac's house and
had just been shouted at, as usual, by Mum (TAKE YOUR
BOOTS OFF) when I heard a taxi grinding up the drive and
soon after, our bell being rung. I was still in the foyer, so
I opened the door and *there she was,* all five feet one of
her, with two gi-normous trunks. I did not know what to
say, but she said, "I am your Great-Aunt Emma. You must
be Tim," and I mumbled something about calling Mother,
but Mum had heard the bell and came hurtling along the
corridor shouting, "If it's the Guides, it must wait till
Tuesday and if it's Mac, tell him to TAKE HIS BOOTS OFF."
When she goes to heaven, she will say this to all the
archangels.

I said, "It's Great-Aunt Emma, Mum; were you expecting?—" But she simply said, "*Most* amusing, you *witty*
lad!" in her Wednesday matinée voice and went racing
past on her way to the kitchen. Then she caught a glimpse
of Aunt Emma and stopped in her tracks and came to the

doorway. "*Who?*" she said. "Great-Aunt *who?*" I could see she was completely taken aback and had never heard of GAE, as I will henceforth refer to Great-Aunt Emma, as she is bound to figure largely in these pages from now on.

GAE said, "You remember me, Millie!" but Mum could only see a vague shape and replied, "Oh dear, I am afraid I don't quite remember—" Then I switched on the porch light and Mum could see GAE properly. GAE leaned forward and said again, "You remember me, Millie!" and this time it registered and Mum cried out, "Great-Aunt Emma! Oh, do come in, you must be freezing. Tim, help with the luggage!"

So we got her inside and she is rather a queer old party. Very short, with a hat with a veil, and gloves, and a way of smiling vaguely. Her teeth are very good (false?) and she is very neat. Her shoes hardly have creases in them over the instep, as if she never walked, yet she is quite spry considering her age, and soon she and Mum were chattering away about the trip and so on. At first Mum didn't seem quite with the situation. I could tell she was faking a lot, but she is such a good faker (unlike Father) that only an outsider could have told that she was a bit baffled by GAE. Anyhow, this soon passed. I saw her (Mum) wipe the back of her hand across her brow, which is always a sign that her mind is now made up and Into Action! After another few minutes you could have sworn that Mum had been expecting GAE for the last two weeks, that the bed was aired, and so on. She is very good at that sort of thing.

Then Father and Beth came in from feeding the rabbits. He made a complete mess of it as usual, saying all the wrong things and making it quite clear that he hadn't a clue about the very existence of Great Aunt. But she fixed him with her beady eye, and grinned, and said, "You remember me, Edward!" And he reentered the twentieth century in great style, pouring everyone sherry. He gave Beth (who is nine) as much sherry as me (eleven) which is typical. Beth was as ever the Outstanding Social Success and shook hands and said, "Oh what a lovely surprise," and looked more like a TV ad than ever. I suppose it's a graceful accomplishment, but it's also the mark of a little cow. She swallowed the sherry pretty fast and went across to pour herself some more, but Mum caught her eye and said "Beth. . . !" and that was the end of that. I got another half glass later. It is quite good sherry, a Manzanilla.

Mum drew me aside and of course it was me that had to go and put hot-water bottles in the spare bed and turn on the heaters and so on to get the room ready for GAE. When I got back to the living room they were all talking away. GAE obviously has a knack for social chitchat, she just asks questions that set people talking again. When I came in, she said, "Tim, are you old enough to smoke?" I said no, of course, although I have smoked (what a ridiculous habit). She said, "I am so glad, now I won't have to be polite and offer you one of these horrid things, I have only four left." She pulled out a packet of Gauloises and lit one—she had already had one, the stub was in an ashtray—and said, "Let me see, are you fourteen or fifteen, Tim?"

I felt myself turning pink at this ridiculous question and mumbled, "Eleven. Nearly twelve." Sure enough, Beth said, "But he's old enough to shave, Aunt Emma!" in her

Sweet Little Girl voice, and everyone began to say, What shave? When shave? Why shave? Who shave? How shave? just as Beth intended. What makes it all worse is that I tried Father's shaving things that time simply out of curiosity, not to prove myself a great hairy man or anything stupid like that. But of course, as Father is always reminding me, WAW, Women Always Win.

Anyhow, what an absurd thing to ask me if I am fourteen or fifteen, quite obviously I am not. If GAE thought she was flattering me, wrong guess. I tried to cover up by asking her how old she was. Beth murmured, "How rude" —another point to her—but GAE said, "I have been sixtynine now for more years that I care to remember," and everyone laughed politely.

So it went on like that and she eventually went off to bed in high style. Thank heaven she is not a kisser, just a peck-on-the-cheeker. When Aunt Lillian was here, saying good night was like those old movies with sobbing violins.

Will get Beth somehow.

January 15

Got Beth over hogging black cherry jam—none left for breakfast. Kid stuff, but A Man Must Do What A Man Must Do. Father packing jeep with cameras and gear for crypt photos, wish he would take me, it's the best part of the cathedral, terrific spooky smell. He was in a panic because he'd messed up the lighting gear as usual and GAE kept asking questions. Antiquated old gear he bought years ago, weighing a ton.

Memo—push catalogues of Japanese electronics under his nose again.

GAE no fool. I wonder how old she really is? Very alert and always asking questions, most of them good. Asked Father WHY he wanted to know about Roman settlement below crypt and he lost another three minutes telling her. Most women merely think his work Quaint, like that woman who kept saying, "*So historical!*" but GAE wants to know what it's all for. Kept asking even when Father gone, so not just faking.

GAE asked where she could get more French cigarettes, saw Mum flinch (though she does not mind them as much as ordinary fags). Told her only one place, Tillots in the village, and even then she would be lucky (she was—they did stock them). She said would I take her, had to say yes. So we walked there, me dreading slow tottering steps and having to hang back. But she kept going at a fair pace. Very cold, nose dripping (mine, not hers—she didn't even mention cold). Funny really, she wore black long coat, black shoes, black hat with fur and veil again. Said it kept her face warm. I said something about the early days of motoring and women wearing veils then but she said she didn't remember and started asking me about cars. What is a sports car for? she asked, and I said, to go faster. How much faster? I said not really much faster, in fact some sedans were faster than some sports cars. Then why did people buy sports cars? Etc., etc. Lots more of this sort. Questions that made me think. I told her about electric cars but GAE said she hates anything electric, which is one of the odd, old-ladyish things about her. She seems to think that anything electrical could *leak* electricity . . . she flinches away from electric fires, irons, anything.

Funny that she asks all these questions at her age. I suppose old people get a second wind when they start looking at life all over again and asking all the questions they didn't ask when they were young. She never talks about the past.

All in all, rather enjoyed the walk and certainly she's a good goer—quite unpuffed on return, lit a Gauloise and read paper right through without a further word.

Father back early in temper, lighting gear failed as I predicted. Gave him Japanese catalogues. This time he may actually look at them.

January 20

Muscle Beach * this morning, Father a bit hearty, saying, "Swimming in January! There's luxury!" Beth as usual moaning and ending up by crying "It's NOT luxury! It's NOT luxury!" which made Father and me laugh. We stripped and dived in, horrible anticipation but very nice once done. Water 67°. Father plowing up and down doing his 30 lengths, very stern and dutiful, but must admit he looks better than most men of his age. For example, cannot imagine Dr. Parry (six years younger than Father) stripped to the buff, must be obscene. Physician, heal thyself.

Beth doing her amazing breaststroke, head and bottom sticking out of water, mouth going "Pouf! Pouf!," eyes closed most of the time.

I did length underwater, then two lengths = 50 feet. Nearly burst lungs.

Mother as usual found excuse, did not come. Yet she is

* Muscle Beach—the Carpenters' swimming pool, built by Mr. Carpenter. It has a removable glass roof and is heated for winter use. The pool is Mr. Carpenter's greatest luxury, the only item, he says, on which he has ever spent more than he can afford—and the only thing, his work apart, about which he is somewhat fanatical and insistent. He uses the pool daily and makes it plain that he expects the family to follow his example at weekends, even in darkest winter.

far best swimmer. My theory—she never really approves of the naked bit. Is it her appendicitis scar? Probably. She is quite vain and I don't blame her as very pretty considering age (34). She moans about the scar—surgeon was a butcher etc., etc.—but not seriously. But she does mention it. I read an article in the paper the other day that said all this modern thing about families romping around naked and unashamed was a snare and a delusion. I must say I never thought about it at all, the swimming pool was just a thing we had and it's always been there—since I was four, anyhow—and you don't wear clothes in your own swimming pool although you do in someone else's or on the beach. No one in our house goes around naked indoors or leaves bathroom door open. But since the Permissive Scene came on, you can't even brush your teeth without feeling that you've got to prove something. I wish I was Father, who simply doesn't comment—just does what he wants to do. But of course, even that's all changed now because of GAE, viz—

There we are splashing in the pool when—*ker-boing!*—door opens, icy blast ruffles water, and lo! GAE has come among us, wearing boots and mild grin! All is instantly confusion! The great traditions hallowed by the Carpenter family are shaken to their foundations!—particularly the tradition whereby Muscle Beach = unembarrassed nudists. Beth is least affected—she merely says *Eeek!,* then recovers herself and goes on with her rotten breaststroke, this time with her eyes open to see how dear Papa and dear Brother take the situation.

I zoom out of the pool at the far end and slide like a seal into a towel in one easy movement. So I am now unnaked and therefore unashamed. Not trendy, but true.

But Father is visibly taken aback. He stops swimming, stands in the middle of the pool and says, "Oh." Then he adds, "Aunt Emma. Oh. Good morning." And, trying to look unconcerned, completes his thirty lengths. But he's concerned all right, because instead of doing racing turns at either end, which he learned with great labor from the swimmers on TV, he now turns in the modest amateur hand-push manner: the difference being that the amateur manner just causes a swirl of water around his shoulder whereas the racing turn shows his *bottom*.

At last he can swim no longer and once again he stands in the middle of the pool and says, in an abnormally normal voice, "Oh, good morning, Aunt Emma. You're up bright and early."

She looks out through the glass overhead as if to check the truth of his statement and replies, "Yes indeed"—then calmly sits down and stares at Father, waiting for him to say something else.

Taking the bull by the horns, he says, "Well, [cough cough], that's enough swimming for me, hum hum, I think I will get out now."

Aunt Emma says, "Yes indeed."

Father's eyes flick first to Beth, who deliberately turns her back on him and duck-dives; then to me—but I pretend to have my arms caught in a sweater. Seeing that he will get no support from his nearest and dearest, Father says, loud and clear, "You must leave now, Aunt Emma, I'm getting out."

"Oh," says Aunt Emma, the grin fading. "Why?"

"Because I'm not wearing anything!" Father grates.

"I should hope not," says Aunt Emma. *"It would only get wet!"*

I was going to go on to examine this situation in depth, but it's too good to spoil and I am sleepy. So I will leave him in the water, facing Aunt Emma (still seated) and laugh myself to sleep.

January 21

Will continue with the events of Saturday (yesterday) as not much doing today. (Incidentally, GAE's footprints in the snow are interesting. Our footprints lead straight to and from the pool. Hers make a long detour around the filtration unit—with its *electric* pump and *electric* humming noise!)

Father in very good form about the Aunt Emma "get wet" story, and made Mum laugh a lot when GAE had gone for her afternoon rest. We were still sitting around the lunch table. Mum said something about it showing what a good sense of humor GAE has, but Beth interrupted her and said, "Oh no! She was quite serious, she really meant it."

I saw Father look puzzled, then Mum said, "Beth, you don't live to the age of seventy-something without knowing the existence of *bathing suits*." But Beth said, "'She meant it, she was quite embarrassed when Father told her to go."

So Father explained to Beth what was meant by a dry sense of humor and said GAE was being drily funny, which caused Beth to make the obvious joke about everyone being wet at the time, etc., etc., etc. The subject was dropped.

Thinking about it later, I believe Beth was right—that GAE really was serious when she made her "joke." But of course that's impossible. Not that it matters one way or the other.

January 22

Yet another "Emmanation," as we now wittily describe
strange remarks made by GAE. Mac's mother called to ask
where was Mac (he was with me, backwashing the pool
filter). So Mum called us into the house and GAE came in
and we had to introduce GAE to Mrs. Rainier. Mum said,
"Great-Aunt Emma, let me introduce Mrs. Rainier, our
nicest neighbor," etc., etc., and Mrs. Rainier said, "Oh,
how interesting, you never told me you had a great-aunt,
Millie!" and GAE said, "Oh, you remember me, Mrs.
Rainier, you remember me" (which seems to be GAE's
formula when being introduced) and then Beth came in
and said, "*I* don't remember you, Aunt Emma, not properly. Only Grandma, I knew her, but Mum never told us
about you!"

There was an awkward pause, then Mum wiped her
hand across her forehead and started talking about cakes
and a failure she had just had and would we all please
eat the good bits. The cake was brought in. It looked OK
but burned. Beth was being the perfect TV kiddie and
saying, "Oh, how perfectly scrumptious," etc., etc. Then
she said, "I love the smoky taste of the burn. All cakes
should be smoked, shouldn't they?"

Mrs. Rainier, making up to the pest, said, "I so agree, ha
ha, cakes should be smoked, they really should, ha ha,
like herrings!"

At which GAE said, "Oh, Mrs. Rainer, you must think me so rude!"—and offered her a box of matches!

Reading this over, I suppose it's not so funny after all and I must stop using "and" all the time to link sentences. But it was the way GAE said it—deadly serious. Perhaps she has got the famous dry sense of humor.

Beth has a point. I wonder why we were never told about GAE by Grandma when she was alive, or by Mum. Perhaps we were told and I did not listen. Mrs. Rainier seemed to know all about her once they'd started talking.

February 2

Father has actually bought Tasaki lighting gear! As usual,
is very pleased with himself and prone to explain it to me
as if I wasn't the one that made him buy it in the first
place. But suddenly caught himself doing this and very
graciously said, "Well, it was your idea really, Tim. I tell
you what. Come to the crypt tomorrow and be Lighting
Technician. Mind you, you'll have to carry it, I don't see
why I should have to lug it around," etc., etc.

I said, "But it only weighs fifteen pounds, that's one of
the selling points I was telling you about!"

He said, "Then why moan about carrying it?"

I fell into the trap and said, "I wasn't moaning—" And
he chuckled and said, "That's how women argue, you
can't beat it!" and laughed some more.

I quite agree with him, that's women. Even Beth at the
age of nine can do it. So can GAE. Told Father about
GAE and Competitive Spirit: I had scored second goal
and we won 4 to 2, so naturally I was highly pleased and
maybe went on a bit about how we had massacred the
other side, etc., etc., and GAE started asking questions
about why winning mattered so much. I said the whole
point of a game was to establish a winner, it was like a
sort of friendly war. That got us on to wars and all the
obvious arguments—if *they* do this, then *you* have no al-
ternative but to do that, etc., etc. She said that perhaps

history would have come out much the same if all the great battles had been settled by the toss of a coin. I said, you mean you would just accept invasion, not fight back? She said yes. So I leaned forward and took her packet of cigarettes and placed them on top of the grandfather clock where she could never reach them and sat down again and grinned at her.

Instead of taking it as a joke, she exhibited anger. She got really cross. "It's only an invasion, Aunt Emma," I said, "only an invasion. Why fight it?"

At that moment Mum came in and Aunt Emma said, "Tim is being rude and unkind," etc., etc. I said, "Oh! An appeal to the United Nations!" Aunt Emma said, *"I insist that you give me back those cigarettes!"* "Then it's war?" I replied. Anyhow, Mum gave her the cigarettes and all was peace and light. Just as well because GAE was looking upset and I was feeling a bit stupid. Later I said sorry.

Father said, "There you are. Never argue theories with a woman. They can't see farther than personalities and in any case, WAW."

I find I am writing very slangily. Various uses of "etc." and lazy use of "and." *Memo: if you are going to write this much, even in a diary, you might as well write it right.*

February 3

Now Beth is at it, doing what Father and I agreed to call Weathercocking—that is, you just disregard the facts and main lines of an argument, and come in from any point of the compass that suits you. If you were north one minute you can be south the next and still expect to win. All part of the WAW phenomenon.

Beth has taken an aversion to Great-Aunt Emma. All of a sudden she simply hates the poor old girl. There was a slight scene last night about kissing GAE good night. Beth just smiled and waved instead of kissing. Mum said something, Beth kissed GAE and then left the room, giving me a Look as she passed. Later I asked what she had been pulling faces for and she said, "Ugh! I hate kissing her, kissing Aunt Emma makes me want to puke!" etc., etc. I said, was it the feeling of her skin (which is a bit odd, I must admit—much too smooth and soft—but that's old age for you, one cannot help getting pouchy). Beth said, Poo, ugh, no, it wasn't that, it was because GAE *does not smell!!!* I sat back and prepared for some weathercocking, viz.—

"You say she does not smell?"

"Yes, that's right, it's all wrong. Ugh, poo," etc., etc.

"But she smokes all the time, so she must smell."

"Oh yes, but that's only her cigarettes, that's not what I mean."

"But French cigarettes have a very strong smell."

"Oh yes, I like the smell of French cigarettes. It's *her* smell I can't stand."

"But you just said she *doesn't* smell."

"Yes, it's disgusting, ugh, poo; that's why I can't stand kissing her goodnight, stupid!"

"But you didn't like that babysitter, Winnie What's-her-name, because she *did* smell."

"Well, that's not as bad as not smelling, how could it be? . . ."

Beat that for weathercocking. And Beth is only nine. By the time she is grown up, she will be fifty times as hopeless.

February 6

Beth nuts, weather freezing, GAE disaster!

This winter worst in several years, snow again yesterday, about an inch, and frost is apparently here forever. Even Father looking a bit blue-faced on way to and from pool.

GAE disaster! Poor old thing slipped on ice and fell down heavily when walking to bird feeder with bacon scraps. I was at school, did not see, but apparently lay there for a little time until Beth rushed out and started to get her up.

Then for no reason whatsoever, Beth let her fall again and raced indoors white-faced and shaking and would not say a word—not that there was much time for words, with GAE still lying there. So Mum went out and got her to her feet and indoors. GAE now has right wrist wrapped in bandages and sits in wing chair smoking French cigarettes and trying to do the crossword, which she is very bad at, particularly the obvious clues. Good at spotting anagrams, though.

"Right wrist wrapped" a tongue-twister? "Nicely white lightly wrapped wrist" . . . "Lily's right wrist wrapped lightly."

Beth has now gone into the opposite of her TV Sweetie act and refuses to say anything to anyone about anything —palely pudding-faced with eyes like holes in the snow.

28

Tried to be nice to her this evening (mending her pen) and carefully broached the subject of GAE—but Beth screamed, "Shut up! Shut up! Shut up!" and ran to her room. Seemed quite all right later but noticed how cunningly she tried to avoid kissing GAE goodnight. Beth went over to her, placed her hand on GAE's wrist and exerted slight "accidental" pressure (hoping GAE would say Ouch and thus Beth could make speedy exit). But GAE took no notice, said, "Goodnight, Bethy!" and Beth had to kiss her after all. Beth looked very sick as she walked out and serves her right for being too clever and complicated about everything. Last time we had pale-pudding-face act, long-term, was when Mac frightened her with fireworks, November 5.

Am deputy skipper for Saturday's away match, not that it matters.

Cannot think what Beth has against GAE. Also cannot be bothered to think about it. GAE a bit boring, this questions thing of hers goes on too much. She is always asking questions and some of the questions are so stupid or mock-stupid or whatever. I think she puts on a Dear Little Old Lady performance (1) to gain attention (although she is not a limelight hogger like, say, Aunt Lillian), (2) to prove she is still young and sprightly, (3) because her mind is getting a little perforated, like a Swiss cheese.

She went on this evening about Sleep, of all things. How strange, she said, that we have to sleep each night. What *is* sleep? How did trees sleep? And oceans? And continents? As there are obvious answers to the first two questions, it was boring to have to listen to Father giving

29

them. And as there are no real answers to the last two questions, I wish she hadn't asked them because it got Mum and Father talking about balances of power, the decline of the West, the rise of the East and all the rest of it.

Like the time there were two dogs at the end of our garden. One was Mrs. Folger's bitch and the dog (unknown) was trying to mount her. GAE immediately burst out with, "Oh! How strange! What is that dog trying to do to the other dog?" at the top of her voice—this in front of all the family and Mac—and for that matter Beth, but she is a hardened rabbit and guinea-pig breeder. Anyhow, someone told her what the dogs were doing and you'd have thought she would have shut up and left it alone. But no, she had to go on and on, asking more and more questions covering the whole animal kingdom and the human race as well. Perhaps she has some antiquated notion about Bringing Things Out into the Open for the Sake of the Children or perhaps she has rotten eyesight and wanted to cover up what she thought to be a goof. But it would have been far better if she had just shut up and smoked another cigarette.

February 8

Beth being stupid and embarrassing again today with
GAE. Asking GAE questions about Granny—Were they
very fond of each other when they were children? What
games did they play? etc., etc., etc. GAE was trying to
answer by turning the questions—"Oh, it was a long time
ago, dear. . . . What is *your* favorite game?" But Beth very
persistent. At last Mum must have overheard because she
called us into kitchen and told us not to pester GAE.
Mum said GAE might be very upset by even least mention of Granny, for sisters can be very close and when
Granny died, who knows what effect it had on GAE, etc.

So Beth did the right thing and went up to GAE saying
(in her best TV-commercial way), "Oh, Aunt Emma, I'm
sorry if I ask too many questions. I hope I didn't upset
you," etc., etc. GAE replying, "No, not at all" [smile
smile]. Beth proceeded to overcook the whole thing by
saying, "Oh, I am glad you are smiling, that proves you
are not cross. *I must call you my Grinny Granny!*"

This so sickening that I nearly brought up my lunch on
the best rug—Beth only needs a lisp to make herself quite
unbearable ("I mutht call you my Gwinny Gwanny").
But GAE (presumably I must now write of her as GG—
joke about the Old Gray Mare coming up, Ho Ho), highly
pleased, grinning more than ever, and Beth like the TV

31

Kute Kid who gets the chocolate cookie with the yummy-yummy-O-my-tummy marshmallow filling.

If I say anything of this to Mac, he gets all gruff and silly—he likes Beth a lot although she is only nine, and wants to do the Big Brother act. If he actually had a kid sister he'd know different, as I keep telling him, but he only goes Strong and Silent.

GAE got working on Mac today and said, "So you and Tim are friends? Really friends, you really are friends? Great friends?" etc., etc. What can you do except look stupid and mumble. But she went on and on asking about friends—would a friend do this if such and such happened, how could you be sure if a Great Friend, etc., etc., ad nauseam. The Quaint Old Lady bit.

We lost 3 to 1 to Millhouse, thanks almost entirely to Cutler's useless center-half play. I got six out of ten for English Comp. and (as usual) the comment TOO SLANGY. The bike's front tire is flat.

Altogether a rotten day.

February 9

This is not easy to write. I know I annoy Beth all the time and make jokes about WAW and so on and she is after all only a nine-year-old (but soon to be ten)—but she is nothing like such a fool as I like to make her out to be and if she is a liar, she is doing it very well—even crying with the lying. I don't know what to make of it.

She was sitting in her room and refusing to come down. Eventually Mum sent me up to tell Beth that dinner was nearly on the table and that she really must come down. I crashed into Beth's room and said, "Oh, come on, Beth, it's dinnertime and I've had to come all the way upstairs," etc., etc. She just burst into tears and said she wasn't coming down, she refused to come down. Leave me alone, and so on.

She looked so awful that I didn't start on her in the usual way but tried to be nice—What's wrong? Did something happen at school? Aren't you well? She said, "No, no, it's her—Grinny! It's Grinny!" Anyhow, Mum was standing at the foot of the stairs yelling for us to come down, so I pulled her (Beth) to her feet and said, "Will you tell me after?" and she replied, "Yes, but only if you promise!" Which means of course promise not to tell anyone else.

She was quiet and white at dinner but I don't think anyone paid much attention as there were two men from the site, a stonemason and a photographer, eating with us and they and Father kept talking shop at the top of their voices all the time. Beth ate as much as usual. But as soon as the meal was over and we had cleared the dishes, she tugged at my arm and made me go back with her to her room.

She said, "I've been dying to tell someone, but they'll only laugh. Will you laugh?" I said no. She said, "Do you think I am just a stupid little girl or don't you? Because I'm not." She started crying again so I gave her the old hug-and-kiss treatment, which I don't often do, so when I do do it it works all the better (*do do it it* is like a word puzzle). It worked now—she stopped crying, stared me straight in the face and said—

"*Grinny's not real.*"

I said, "Oh." I was disappointed in her for being so childish, actually.

She said, "Yes, I knew you would take it like that, you just think I'm stupid, but I am not. *Grinny is not real*, she's not a real person at all."

It went on like this for a little while, then I said, "Tell me exactly and precisely what you are talking about and no fooling around, and above all do not cry."

She said, "You remember the day she fell down on the ice and hurt herself?" I said yes. "Well, I was the first one there, I was there just about a second after she did it; she was still lying on the ground and I was there beside her. And I saw something you will never believe, never!"

I said what was it and I would try to believe her.

She said, "Something horrible, it was *horrible!* I saw her wrist actually broken and the bone sticking out!"

I replied, "That's impossible. Do be reasonable, she was

34

perfectly all right quite soon after. If you break your wrist it is very serious, it takes weeks or months to mend. Particularly if you are old. And it is very painful, agony, in fact. So you just couldn't have seen it, Beth, you only thought you saw it because you have a good imagination."

Beth said, "I haven't got a good imagination, Penny writes much better essays than I do and so does Sue. I saw it, I saw it, I saw it!"

So I made her tell me just what it was she saw. She started off by repeating that I would never believe her and so on, but in the end it came down to this—I am choosing my words very carefully so as not to distort what she said—

"She was lying on the ground in a heap. She was not groaning or moaning, just lying there and kicking her legs, trying to get up. I went close to her and got hold of her elbow so that I could help pull her up. She did not say anything to me, like 'Help me' or 'My wrist hurts'— she just tried to get up. When I seized her elbow, I saw her wrist. The hand was dangling. The wrist was so badly broken that the skin was all cut open in a gash and the bones were showing."

I told Beth I understood all this, but she seemed unwilling to go on. She looked at me and wailed, "Oh, it's no good, you'll never believe me!" but I made her go on. She said:

"The skin was gashed open but there was no blood. The bones stuck out but they were not made of real bone— they were made of shiny steel!"

I have these words right. Beth did say what I have written. I am quite certain about asking her what sort of

35

bones, what sort of steel and so on. Her answers were, that the steel was silvery shiny and that the bones looked smaller than proper bones—more like umbrella ribs. When I asked her what umbrella ribs look like, she answered (correctly) that they are made of channels of steel, not solid rods like knitting needles. She said that GAE's bones were in "little collections" of these steel ribs and that the skin had been torn by a few of the ribs breaking away from a main cluster and coming through the skin.

So I asked her again about the absence of blood and she was positive. She said there was no blood, no blood at all, the skin was just split open. I asked her what color the skin was and she said the same color outside as in. I said, well, there must have been meaty stuff where the bones were, but she said no. There was nothing but the steel ribs and that the skin was just a thick layer "like the fat on a mutton chop before it is cooked," but with a tear in it.

I thought of all kinds of reasons for her telling this story, ranging from my linocut set, which has very sharp (= frightening) gouges, some of them the same section as umbrella ribs; right down to playing in the garden when we were much younger with an old tattered umbrella, all spokes and no cover (it was pelting with rain and we were making a joke of the useless umbrella, etc., etc.).

As I was thinking of all the things that might have caused Beth to think she saw what she said she saw, she began again. "I saw her wrist mend! I saw it heal itself!" she said.

I must say, this gave me goose pimples. I said, "What do you mean?" And Beth told me that as she watched, *the skin came together over the broken bones, leaving a bump covering the breaks.* That was when Beth became really frightened and ran inside.

I said to her, "You know that people actually can have metal bones?" She said, "Oh, yes, I've always known that and so have you. Father nearly had one, you remember." I did remember—he broke a bone and the hospital thought that he might have to have a steel rod inserted to pin the bone. In the end he didn't. Some people do, however, and it may be permanent. A man in the village has a metal plate in his skull.

So it is no good me trying to pretend that Beth has some fixation or other about bones and umbrella ribs because she simply hasn't. Cream, coffee, chocolates, chicken and stuffing—she's certainly got fixations about them. But not people's bones.

By now she was saying, "I told you! I knew all along you wouldn't believe me!" and preparing to have a good cry again. I managed to avoid this by more kiss-and-hug treatment and in the end I said, "All right, so Grinny has an artificial arm, let's say, made by some super surgeon. For all we know, she's got false teeth, wears a wig, has a cork leg and a glass eye. Fine! But what difference does it make? Why get upset and refuse to kiss her goodnight and all the rest of it?"

Beth set up a great howl and shouted, "Oh, how can you be so stupid! It's nothing to do with false legs and glass eyes—IT'S BECAUSE SHE'S NOT REAL, that's why I can't stand her, NONE OF HER IS REAL!"

She was making such a row that I said, "All right, all right, I understand now. And then of course you don't like the way she smells and it all adds up in your mind—"

Beth went very white and said, "Yes, and she doesn't smell of anything, that's another thing! And she asks those stupid questions! And she's frightened of electricity! It all proves it, she's not real!"

I quieted her down eventually (she had started crying again in a very big way) and let her come into my room while I did my homework. She was fairly happy by bedtime. But I must admit she has put a scare into me. I am writing this rather late and I keep expecting a crack to appear in the wall, then a hole, then a metal hand come through the plaster. That sort of thing. A good story might be written about a metal hand.

I just do not know what to make of it all. Beth's only a little girl but she is *not* an idiot.

February 10

Big family row today, BAM, POWIE, ECHHHH!—Beth the cause. Would not eat her breakfast, doing her White-faced Orphan act; "Oh, no, Mama, I am not unwell, I am quite all right, it is just that I am not hungry." Mum slamming buttered toast down in front of her and saying, "Look, you little viper, eat this toast or I will hang you from a hook over a slow fire," etc., etc. Lurid imagery. Father moaning, "For heaven's sake shut UP! Where are those Canadian boots of mine? Blast Beth, I must have dry feet." I felt rather sorry for Beth in a way because for once in a million years she could actually have slept badly because of Grinny and the metal bones. Eventually she nibbled at the toast and made a disgusting sick noise and deposited what she had chewed on the plate. Mum instantly all sympathy and tenderness, but Father unexpectedly went ape and shouted, "Disgusting! What the devil do you mean by—" etc., etc.

At this moment, Mac entered looking wholesome and fresh-faced. He had come to pick me up. He instantly sized up the situation and went to work on it with his usual nasty skill. That is what I like about Mac; he is very quick on the uptake. Even though he likes Beth, he couldn't resist pushing things a little farther. He kept being Cheerful and Nice—he's very good at that—while Mum fumed and Father erupted in grunts and snarls and Beth looked puke-y. Puky? Pukey? Mac said, "Gosh! What super marmalade, Beth! We never have the chunky stuff at home! Gosh, you are lucky!" and so on, and Beth looked sicker and sicker. Eventually she fled from the room, wailing. I thought he was overdoing it with the "Goshes," and Father suspected him too, but Father likes Mac because Mac genuinely enjoys swimming even when the water is cold, unlike us, who do it from a sense of duty toward something or other.

Anyhow, Mum offered Mac a cup of coffee and deliberately put only one spoonful of sugar in it to let him know that she was on to him and Father read the paper very busily, not looking up. Beth then came back looking rabbit-eyed from a quick cry and Mac said, "Here's your toast and marmalade, Beth, it's still OK. Eat hearty!"

This was pushing his luck. Beth scooped up the toast and flung it at him shouting, "Pig! Beast! Swine!" etc., etc. The toast missed Mac and hit the wall, where it slowly slid down because of the stickiness of the marmalade. It was a marvelous sight, I could not help laughing, but Father was really angry and yelled, "Get out, the whole bloody lot of you!" and went to get a dishcloth to wipe the wall. He made it too wet and now the wallpaper is coming up in a big blister.

I cannot think why I bother to write all this down, it is so childish and futile. Or perhaps I can think why after all. The point is, that GAE was ABOUT TO COME DOWN FOR BREAKFAST. (Astounding, my dear Holmes! But I confess, I remain baffled. Pray be more explicit. . . .) What I mean is this. Grinny has got us all on the run. The mere fact of EXPECTING her to enter the dining room is enough to put everyone on edge. Beth was already on edge, of course, and who can blame her? But Mum and Father are feeling it too, they do not like the continued presence of Grinny in the house. Before she came, we used to have our breakfasts in a surly but comfortable silence, with Father chomping away and reading the papers, Mum vaguely instructing us in how to be better Citizens of the Future ("Well, if you think I am going to clean your shoes for you, think again, you will not leave this house until those shoes are cleaned," etc., etc), Beth practicing her feminine wiles and me trying to eat as much as possible without exposing my fingernails ("You are *not* leaving this house with cabbages growing from your filthy fingers. Edward, *say* something, he is *your* son," etc.).

In short, we were quite comfortable and ordinary. But now at breakfast and at many other times of the day, we are all in some funny way awaiting the arrival of Grinny. Father will make to rise from his chair, but Grinny will say, "Oh, Edward dear, don't get up"—so Father will grin at Grinny and Grinny will grin at Mum and Mum will smirk at me and I will kick Beth under the table, etc.. etc.

At first I thought this uneasiness was something to do with age. Grinny is a very old lady and we, the family, are used to each other and don't think about each other's ages, we just accept it (except Mum, who is prone to smile as if she had false teeth when it's her birthday. I would hate to be a woman but would not mind being a girl— they get it all their own way for the first twenty years or so).

As I was saying before I so rudely interrupted myself, at first I thought it was just the presence of an old lady, a

foreigner, in our midst. Now I have caught Beth's bug—
"Grinny is not real"—and find myself brooding about her a
lot. But the broken-wrist story is a bit too much. When
Mac and I were on our way to school I said, "Mac, what
do you think of Grinny?" He said, "Queer old party.
Rather you than me."

I said, "What do you mean, queer?"

He replied, "Her Mona Lisa smile. She looks like the cat
that swallowed the canary. As if she knew it all."

I said, "But she doesn't know anything much, that's
what's so annoying about her. She's always asking stupid
questions; you must have noticed."

He said "Yes, she fixes you with her eye and asks all
those questions. . . . What does she live on?" "Food," I
replied. Mac said, "You're so *cute*. I mean, has she any
money? Does she pay you rent or something? Has she an
income?"

I had never thought of this, but am thinking about it
now. I am also thinking about how long she will stay,
why it is that Mum and Father never talk about her going
(they certainly talk about certain of our guests going, and
the sooner the better!) and why it is that even now, after
all this time, nobody ever talks about Grinny's early days
with our Granny.

I have been nice to Beth this evening, but she is still in
a silent and won't-play mood. How strange if Beth were
right and Grinny is not real! And if she isn't a real GAE,
what the hell is she instead?

February 12

Beth now in a very different mood. She has gone all defiant and We Shall Not Be Moved. Strike Action. She now refuses to kiss Grinny goodnight and barely talks to her. Big scenes with Mum, who says, "You must," but Beth just says, "I won't." And she doesn't; I must hand it to her for that.

I talked to her (Beth) about it this evening and you gotta hand it to the little lady, she's convinced herself. Do not confuse me with the facts, my mind is made up, etc., etc. She says, "Grinny is *not* real, she is horrible. I won't have anything to do with her. And that is that."

Grinny takes it very well, just smiles vaguely and lets it pass. She does not attempt to be nice to Beth and strike up conversations. Father hardly notices.

February 18

Re Beth's Operation Grinny (see Feb. 12). Report from all Fronts. Beth still on strike, Mum still saying, "Oh, do see reason," Father still silent, Grinny still grinning, Mac now more curious than anyone but me.

At dinner (Mac with us after soccer) Mac asked her point-blank about earlier days. He did it all very well, the uninstructed youth bowing before the wisdom of old age, etc., etc. Where did she spend her childhood? he asked, and wouldn't let go.

Mum tried to interrupt by saying something or other, I forget what, but Mac kept asking. At last Grinny said, "Oh, the past is over and done with, I never think of the past."

Mac still pressed on and said, "Oh, but surely you must think about your sister, Tim's granny?"

Mum sort of gasped and made a face to shut Mac up, but Grinny replied, "Well, you see, my sister and I were so very different. Quite different. Very close, of course, but quite different." Then she gave a sort of little laugh which could have been embarrassment but which Beth said later was *sinister* (Beth's new word).

Mac said, "But—" and Mum came in very strong saying, "Mac, I would rather you didn't pester Aunt Emma with questions."

Mac said, "But—" again, and Mum said, "More tea, Aunt Emma? More tea, anyone?" And that was that.

Now comes the significant part. An hour or more later, I found Mum in the kitchen and said to her, "Oh, I do wish you had let Mac go on. I was hoping we'd find out." She said, "Go on about what?" I said, "About Aunt Emma's past and about Granny and everything."

She looked me straight in the eye and said, "What are you talking about? Mac said *what?*" She did this as if she really meant it—as if she really had forgotten the conversation. But she doesn't forget things, she has the usual terrifying WAW memory about anything to do with *people* —what they wore, what they said, etc., etc. Anyhow, I kept on at her a bit more and even said, "Don't you remember telling us not to pester Aunt Emma with questions about Granny?" But either Mum wasn't really hearing me or she was making everything slide out of her mind.

Unless, of course, someone else—Grinny herself!—was making her forget.

Then suddenly Mum looked ill. She put her hand to her head and said, "I'm so tired. My head aches."

I have just reread all this and have realized what a complete fool I am making of myself. Going on like a girl about what *this* one said and what *that* one said and if you want *my* opinion . . . worse than a girl. And all about a perfectly ordinary old lady.

I HEREBY RESOLVE TO SHUT UP ABOUT GRINNY and concentrate on things that matter. I WOULD BE ASHAMED IF THIS DIARY WERE FOUND because it is full of drivel and has nothing that matters. IT IS ALSO APPALLINGLY WRITTEN.

TIMOTHY CARPENTER, TURN OVER A NEW LEAF. TIMOTHY CARPENTER, TURN . . .

February 19

I resolved yesterday to stop writing about Grinny and start writing about something important.

I must break the first promise if only to keep the second.

Something extraordinary happened last night and it concerns Grinny.

I must make sure to get everything in the right order and into plain English.

First the UFO (Unidentified Flying Object). There have been various UFO scares in this district, and I never believed in such nonsense. Now I have changed my mind. I saw a UFO myself. So did Beth and my father.

It happened like this. I prepared to go to bed after writing up my diary at about 12:30, which is very late for me. I suppose I was the last person awake in the house except for one—but more about that later.

I looked out of the window because it was a cold night and I like the look of the moon on frost. The moon was very bright indeed, almost full. Unusually bright—the frost made the whole scene superreal, like a stage set with special pale-blue lighting.

In spite of the brilliance of the light, I saw *it* perfectly distinctly.

When I first saw it, it was fairly near the moon's position in the sky. It was far brighter than the moon and had a yellowish brilliance. I remember thinking how it clashed with the steely blue of the moon. I also remember seeing the yellowish reflections of its light on the frosted grass of the lawn—the sort of effect you get when you look at a boat with a light on it, far out at sea. Only very different, of course, because it made warm, yellowish reflections on the bluish grass.

I had plenty of time to look and all the time I stared at it, my heart was going faster and faster. So I was excited, but only physically, not mentally. I remember thinking, "If it stays there much longer, I will be able to get Father, and he can agree with me about what I am seeing."

It *did* stay in position—or rather, it traveled so slowly that I had to keep checking the gap between It and the moon's position. It went very slowly *and not steadily*. Sometimes it paused. When it started to move again, it made *an oval luminous halo or nimbus*. I think (and so does Father) that it was flying within our atmosphere and this nimbus was the result of very cold air being disturbed by the thrust and/or movement of It—rather like the contrails (condensation trails) you get from ordinary aircraft.

Without taking my eyes off it, I moved away from the window and felt behind me for my telescope, which is hung on two hooks on the wall. It is not a high-power instrument, just a World War Two military telescope used for artillery spotting and so on. But it does give a very sharp image, as good as the best modern field glasses, Father says. I felt for and found the telescope and, constantly keeping my eyes on it, pulled the telescope into rough focus. Then I lowered the window and rested the telescope on the frame to steady it and the UFO just *jumped* into focus!

I could see nearly everything about it. I could even see that it was revolving slowly, in a clockwise direction, and had several "windows" or vents. I could very easily see its halo or nimbus, which looked like cirrus cloud (the very high, veillike cloud).

At this moment, I heard my parents' bedroom door open quietly and Father's footsteps padding along the hallway. He was going to the bathroom. I ran backward to my door, still keeping my eyes on It, and called him. He said, "Oh, aren't you asleep? *Now* what's the trouble?" and came rather grumpily into my room.

He said, "What are you doing in the dark?" and turned the light on. (I forgot to mention that I had turned the light out the better to see the moonlit frost.) I said, "Turn it off! Quickly! Come over here!"

He was still saying things rather crossly and sleepily but I said, "Look! Up there, in the sky! Look through the telescope!"

He looked for a long time and said, "My God!" Then he said, "Pinch my arm, Tim." I thought he was joking but he was not, so I pinched him fairly hard. He said, "All right, all right! My God!"

A little later he said, "I must get my camera, it should be a cinch to get a picture with the long lens. It can't be far away, you can see it so well, so clearly. . . ."

I said, "What about the police? Shouldn't I telephone them? No one will ever believe us!"

He replied, "I would rather you got the camera—no, I've a better idea, wake your mother and Beth, the more witnesses, the better." Then he changed his mind again and said, "No, don't wake your mother, she was so tired

. . . get Beth, then the camera. Quick as you can."

I said I would and asked if anything was happening (Father was looking through the telescope, not me). He said, "No, it's just moving in occasional lazy spurts, always in the same direction. And each time it moves it makes a mist—"

"Like a nimbus?" I interrupted.

"Yes, I think it's simply condensation, frozen vapor."

Which is exactly what I had thought. Father and I agreed on this point later. Presumably it must have been well within our atmosphere, for there is no moisture to condense in true space.

I got Beth. She wakes very quickly and I could hear her exclaiming while I prodded about behind the desk in Father's study (it is next to their bedroom) looking for his camera case. I found it and took it to him. He was just taking the telescope from Beth, who was murmuring, "A spaceship! It *is* a spaceship!" in an astounded sort of way. Father said, "Can you put the longest lens on, Tim?" but I replied (rather craftily, because I wanted to get back to the telescope), "No, I'd rather you did it, Father, it's safer." So I got the telescope from him while he opened the camera bag and got the body and the long lens out. Then he started swearing mildly, saying, "It's got a blasted color film in, it will be too slow, I'll have to change to black and white—is the thing still there, Tim?"

I said yes and Beth kept tugging at my arm, so I let her have another turn at the telescope.

Suddenly she shouted, "Oh!" and I said, "What's happened?"

She said, "It's gone! Oh, no, it hasn't, it's moved. But it

49

Drawing by Mr. Carpenter. He and his children each made a drawing of the UFO. They then compared their three drawings. Finally, they agreed on the sketch reproduced here.

Many readers may find this drawing shows something familiar. If so, the reason is simple enough: UFO sightings most commonly relate to cigar-shaped, cross-shaped and saucer-shaped craft. The Carpenters say they saw what thousands of others claim to have seen—a "flying saucer."

The Author

50

went so fast. . . ! It just *flashed* away! It's all right, I've got it now. . . ."

Father was still fiddling with the film and trying to keep his eye on It at the same time. I felt sorry for him. Beth announced, "I'm going to get Mummy!" and Father said, "No, don't." I said, "She wasn't well, she had a bad headache—" Beth said, "Can I get Grinny, then?" I said, "Why?" She said, just as Father and I had done, "The more people see it, the better." Then she thought for a moment, shuddered, and said to me, "I'd rather you went to get her if you don't mind" in the sort of polite voice girls use when they intend to pull their femininity on you and make it impossible for you to argue.

I said, "Oh, all right," and went to wake Grinny.

She sleeps in the spare bedroom up another flight of stairs. As I went up these stairs I remember looking out of the little window just at the moment when it suddenly darted off again. It seemed to accelerate instantly—one minute it was going slowly, the next very fast indeed, with no warmup. It traveled some 30° through the sky and stopped in its new position just as suddenly as it had started. A sheet of nimbus enveloped it so that for a moment you could only just see it through the veil. Then the yellowish lights were there again, just as before.

I then went on again up the stairs, walking very quietly so as not to disturb Mum, who was below me. I opened the door of Grinny's room. . . .

At first I just couldn't take it in. I couldn't believe it. So I was not frightened, only shocked.

Grinny was lying flat on her back on the bed, with her arms by her side above the covers. She was rigid and still, like a corpse or an Egyptian mummy. *But she was luminous.* There was even a faint glow through the bedclothes. I remember thinking in a matter-of-fact sort of way, "She doesn't seem to need much covering. Just one blanket . . ." Because of course the light couldn't have passed through several blankets.

I went closer—I wasn't frightened yet—and saw another thing: *her eyes were wide open.* She was staring at the ceiling, staring at nothing. And her eyes were lit up from inside, like water when you put the lens of a lit flashlight in it. Her mouth was open. She was grinning. I don't mean she was making the movement of smiling, I mean her mouth was set in a grin. And from her open mouth I thought I heard a slight fluttering, twittering sound. But it might have been my own heartbeat.

I think it was the reflection of her luminosity on her teeth that made me give a sort of scream.

Then things happened very quickly. She awoke when I screamed or whatever noise it was. As she awoke, her luminosity faded, just like *that.* At the same instant, I heard Father shouting and heard his footsteps and Beth's in the passage. I think he said, "It's gone!" In fact, he must have said this, because at the very moment that Grinny woke up, the spaceship just whipped off into invisibility. I heard Beth answer him and they must have been making excited comments while Grinny came to.

If anyone ever reads all this, they will ask, "But surely you must know exactly what happened within those two or three seconds?"

The answer is no. It is still a bit vague and this is why. Grinny sat up in bed—I remember that she just sat straight up, as if her body were hinged at the base of the spine—and gripped me by the wrist. It was like a claw, her hand. It fastened on me like a parrot's claw, very strong and funny-feeling. Like a clamp.

Anyhow, she clamped me with her hand and then looked me straight in the eye. I remember that her eyes still had a trace of the luminous, lit-from-within look about them. And she was still grinning. And I remember her mouth opening to say something. I remember that quite distinctly. What I cannot remember, however hard I try, is what she said. Everything seemed to go . . . fuzzy. She was there, the room was there, she was speaking, Father and Beth were outside and about to enter—I had a fuzzy impression of all this and still have. Yet I cannot remember what she said.

It wasn't fright that makes me forget. I don't know what it is. I can even remember another thing—when she caught hold of me with her clamplike hand, I remember my wrist trembling in her grip, and thinking to myself how solid and strong her grip was. I was vibrating against something solid, so to speak.

But what she *said* to me—what really *did* happen during the few seconds before Father and Beth came in—well, I just cannot bring it back. I keep searching my memory but it is no good.

Father and Beth came in, very excited, both talking at once. They said that the UFO had just whisked away and gone without a trace, etc., etc. Grinny was full of old-ladyish excitement—she kept saying, "Oh, I *wish* I could have seen it!" and things like that.

I was still feeling a bit blurry or fuzzy and didn't say much. A week ago I had to fight Stannard, who is a very good boxer. He doesn't hit all that hard, but he just seems to get through to you and you can't get through to him. Anyhow, we fought the usual three rounds and he of course was announced the winner, and I went back to the center of the ring to shake hands and so on and so on. What I am getting at is this—after being hit so many times by him, I was quite cheerful and normal and all the rest of it but I did feel a bit cloudy, as if I were watching myself from a distance as I was going through the actions.

And that is just how I felt now. As if I were watching myself being Timothy Carpenter.

In the end, everyone went to bed and the house became quiet. I lay awake for a long time. I was trying to work it all out. I could remember seeing Grinny in that horrible luminous state, with her eyes lit up and her teeth glinting. Remember it?—I couldn't forget it! But then what? Had she wiped me out—my memory, I mean? And if she had, why hadn't she done it more completely? Why leave me remembering the luminous bit?

Here is another funny thing. When I try and write about my thoughts, as in the preceding paragraph, I get a sort of mental itch. I just cannot get going. To sort it all out. And I keep getting different ideas about what happened and didn't happen. Mind you, it is very late and I didn't sleep properly last night, of course. Yet I don't feel sleepy. I wish I could get it going. Unscramble it.

February 25

Talked to Beth about Grinny, but didn't tell her very much, as she is already hysterical enough about the subject. I just said, "It was very odd that night before you came into the room." She kept saying, "I told you so, there's something awful about her, I told you so," etc., etc. I kept the pot boiling without letting it boil over—in other words. I kept picking at her, trying to find out her opinions about Grinny. I got her to the point where she listed all the things she doesn't like about Grinny. She was counting them off on her fingers, mouth pursed and her eyes completely circular. Her list amounts to this:

1. G isn't real. Metal bones, etc. She doesn't smell right (or doesn't smell at all).
2. She is frightened of electricity. I really cannot see this one at all. Many perfectly reasonable people are frightened of electricity, gas, losing their keys, going out without their spectacles, etc., etc., etc., etc. Beth, however, says it is *sinister*.
3. She asks stupid questions or makes stupid comments, yet—
4. She is not stupid at all. In fact she is very lively-minded.

5. She keeps *looking* at you, especially when you have no clothes on.

6. She never *says* anything, she only talks.

Points 5 and 6 are fairly new to me. Point 5—she keeps looking at you. . . . I asked Beth what she meant. She was very embarrassed (so was I) but she got it out in pieces in the end. She said that Grinny looked at her all over when she was in the swimming pool and looked at me too. I said Nonsense, but Beth said, "No, it's true. She had a good old *look*. And she asks questions about Sex!"

I couldn't help laughing at this, but Beth flew into a temper and said, "It's all very well for you to laugh, but it's *true*. I know it's ridiculous, but she *does*. She wants to know about me and your dim friend Mac—oh, go on, laugh, but he is fond of me because he hasn't got a sister of his own and his mother isn't all that nice to him and he wants someone pretty *just to smile at him*—"

(I interrupt this flood of Bethism to point out that I think she is absolutely and 100 per cent RIGHT. If Mac could, he would live here and be a Carpenter. His mother is a cold fish and his father is worse and he does like Beth because he sees in her something he hasn't got at home. So WAW, as usual.)

Beth went on to say (this time I won't try and write her own words as they were so rambling) that Grinny looks at Beth and me and anyone else as if they were foreign bodies. She wants to see how they are made, why they are made like that, what effect it has on them and their behavior and so on and so on.

It sounds like nonsense to me but that is what she says.

56

And the puzzling thing is that though I disagree with Beth simply on logic, I *feel* Beth is right. And then, what about the dogs?—the ones mating on the lawn?

Beth's point 6 was that Grinny never *says* anything, she only talks. This is absolutely true and quite obvious. She is like the wise old owl who lived in an oak, the more it saw the less it spoke. But I cannot see that it matters much, there are many people who go through life "not committing themselves." You hear two women in a bus, one does the talking and the other one just says, "She never!" "He didn't!" "Well, it goes to show!" "Imagine that, then!" This woman is the Receiver and the other one is the Sender. If Grinny chooses to play the part of Receiver, that's her affair.

Yet, once again, I can see what Beth means. Grinny never tells you anything about herself, about Granny, about the old days (most old people love talking about the old days) or about anything at all.

In the end, I got into an argument with Beth, which is always fatal because she cannot argue. She just gets passionate or stubborn. This time she became both at once and shouted, "You don't pay any attention to me, you think I'm just stupid. Well, if I'm stupid, so's Grinny, only worse! What about Grinny and the cast-iron chestnut?"

I admit I had quite forgotten it. It happened only last night and did not seem important at the time. But Beth thought it important.

We were having dinner and Mac was with us. Mac and I were talking about the crazes at school—the crazes that sweep the whole place for anything from a week to a term, it might be anything at all. I said to Mac, "I've still got All-time Champion, the cast-iron conker!" He said, "You haven't! What, old Cast-Iron himself? I don't believe you!" etc., etc. Grinny said, "I don't quite understand. . . . What is a conker?"

I was a bit surprised, but explained. She said, "Oh, of course! Conkers! Chestnuts that you hit against each other! And the winner is the one that doesn't break! Oh, yes!"

I went upstairs and got it. Mac said, "It's not quite the chestnut it was, it looks clapped out. But its soul goes marching on."

Grinny was peering at it, so I said, "It's unique, Aunt Emma, it came from the only cast-iron chestnut tree in the world—just over there, by the bottom of our garden! Every chestnut warranted gen-u-ine solid cast iron!"

She reached out her hand and I gave her Old Cast-Iron. She looked at it for some time, turning it over and over, and then, quite shyly, said, "I don't think it really *is* cast iron, Tim . . . it seems to me to be made of vegetable matter, not cast iron at all!"

Then, poker-faced, she handed it back to me.

Was she serious or wasn't she? Beth swears she was.

February 26

We (Beth, Mac and I) have formed the GCG Council to explore Grinny's Credibility Gaps. We are going to do it conscientiously, systematically and artistically, so that we can find out who's fooling who (whom).

The object is to discover (a) is she suffering from lapses of memory—or (b) has she just a very dry sense of humor, so that she pretends to believe impossible things, or not know things she ought to know? (c) Just how far can we push her ignorance, innocence, cunning, dry humor or whatever it is? (d) And if it turns out that there is something odd about her, how can we learn what particular oddity it is?

To fulfill these objectives, we are going deliberately to stage impossibilities among the three of us. That is, we are going to contrive situations that she must react to. When she reacts, we can judge her reactions. When we judge her reactions, we can also come to some sort of conclusion about her "realness" or the opposite.

February 27

The first exposure of Grinny's Credibility Gap came this evening. It was quite unplanned. It happened after dinner. Mac was not with us, which is a pity, but he can take our word for what happened—it was all very simple.

We were talking about last Christmas—what a panic it had been, our presents, etc., etc. Beth was talking about her school Nativity play and she was getting very enthusiastic about it in a rather showing-off sort of way (she had been chosen to play the Virgin Mary and didn't intend us to forget about her starring role). She was being all little-girlish and starry-eyed, rambling on and on, until she came to the point where she said these words—

"—And then they put the baby in my arms and of course I cuddled it and the funny thing was that that was the first time I'd ever really and truly felt like a real, proper mother!"

This was the only part of Beth's sickening speech that Grinny heard—she had been upstairs and was now down with us. Anyhow, Grinny leaned forward and said, "A baby, Beth . . . ? But I never knew! Where is it?"

Beth was thrown for a moment by the sheer idiocy of this question. Then I saw that cunning look come on her face. She said, "Oh, Aunt Emma, you can't expect me to start having babies yet. I mean, it's physically impossible *for at least another year or so.*"

To which Grinny replied, perfectly seriously, "Yes, of course."

Beth said, hammering it home, and glancing at me to make sure I was getting the point, *"When I am ten. Or even eleven."*

Grinny made no answer in particular. She just made some sort of noise of agreement and fumbled with her cigarettes.

Let us recap.

Here we have Beth saying, in effect, "I have had a baby" (at the age of nine) and Grinny saying, "Let me see it." Beth then says, "No, you are mistaken, girls cannot have babies until they are ten or even eleven." Grinny does not quarrel with this. In fact, Grinny does not do anything except look lost and confused.

What are we supposed to make of that?

March 10

News from the GCG.

The next test situation we put Grinny to came about of its own accord. We (the whole family) were talking about the UFO we had seen and Grinny was saying she wished she had seen it; how terrible to have missed such an extraordinary event, etc. Beth looked at the clock and said, "Oh dear, you've just missed some beauties." Now, I knew what she meant, so did everyone but Grinny. Beth meant that half an hour previously, the TV program *Lonespace* had been on the air—and if Grinny had been watching that, she would have seen all kinds of super-deluxe spacecraft, UFO's, etc., because that is what the program is all about. She would also have known that the spacecraft are carefully made models and the actors are puppets, etc., etc.

But Grinny did not know this; she took Beth's remark at face value. Grinny said—very sharply—"Where? When? What spacecraft? What did you see?"

By luck, I managed to catch Beth's eye for a split second and she played it straight when she answered. She said to Grinny, "Oh, the sky is absolutely full of them, Grinny—"

"At certain times of year—" I put in. I meant, of course, when the *Lonespace* series is running.

"That's right, at certain times of year," Beth went on. "Tim and I love watching them, don't we, Tim?"

She said this without a blink, which was clever of her. But then she is always quick to catch on. Grinny was by now taking it still more seriously. I have never seen her look more alert and determined. She said, "How long have you two been seeing them? What did they look like?"

"Two or three years," Beth replied. "That's right, isn't it, Tim?"

I said, "No, even longer than that."

Grinny rapped out, "But that is impossible! I mean, it is most unlikely. . . . What were they like?" She seemed really upset.

I let Beth answer, because I could see she was in the mood. She did it perfectly, picking at a tuft of wool in the carpet and not looking at all interested—just matter-of-fact. "Well, some of them have a lot of jet things at the back, whole clusters of them," she began. "Those ones are often pointed, rather like a dart, and then there's the jets at the back with smoky stuff coming out—"

"Have you seen spaceships like that?" Grinny asked me, leaning forward in her chair.

"Oh, yes. I think they must be the interstellar ones—the really big craft, carrying lots of people—if they *are* people. But then there are several other sorts, aren't there, Beth?"

"Sometimes you get the flattish ones, rather like rays—you know, manta rays, the fish—they go much slower. And they don't leave jet trails, they just *go*."

"And then there are the container-shaped ones," I cut in. "Very elaborate sort of tin cans, some of them linked together with a sort of lattice of steelwork. And you might see ones like huge rings with the living quarters in the middle—"

Grinny was drinking all this in. Once or twice her lips moved as if she were about to say "But—" She asked several more questions about when, where, and how long, but we managed to answer them without giving the game away. She was getting more and more tensed up.

In the end, Mum shouted for Beth to set the table, so she got up and I said, "Oh, I suppose I'd better help," and went with her. This was just as well, because Grinny would soon have forced us to say we saw all these wonderful spacecraft in a TV program called *Lonespace*. As it was, we left her looking very worried indeed.

I am worried too. It is the same old problem. Here is an old woman who can be told by two children that they have often seen things in the sky—elaborate spacecraft of various sorts—and take it all seriously. Very seriously. She was *worried*. I remember that she was particularly worried when we said we had been seeing them *for years*— that was when she said, "But that is impossible!" She looked really worked up then.

Continued tomorrow. Too tired tonight.

March 11

The other trick we played on Grinny worked so well that it means the end of GCG. It worked too well.

This one did not happen by itself. Tim and Beth and I arranged it to test Grinny's reaction to electricity. You will remember that she has always been peculiar about electricity and we wanted to find out more.

So Mac brought a Wimshurst machine to our house. This is an antediluvian device with two big contrarotating wheels and sticks with knobs on the end of them sticking out. You wind the handle, the two wheels turn, static electricity is generated—and you get exciting blue sparks zipping around between the two knobs. My father was delighted when he saw it. He said they had one at his school when he was a boy; it was supposed to teach the children about electricity. He chuckled a lot and wound the handle faster and faster trying to get bigger and better sparks. He said he was amazed to know that such a machine still existed; where did we find it? etc. Mac told him that it was rotting away in a storeroom in the school, which is quite true.

Anyhow, we waited until Father and Mum were somewhere else and carted the ridiculous contraption into the livingroom, where Grinny was. Then we started turning the handle slowly and chattering to each other, hoping to attract Grinny's attention.

Sure enough she started asking all the right questions and we gave her some rather wrong answers. Mac said it was a bacon slicer. I said, "It's not, don't be such a fool. Have you ever seen a bacon slicer like this, Grinny? Really . . . !" She said no, she never had. Beth then said, as arranged, "What *does* a bacon slicer look like, Grinny?" and Grinny gave an evasive answer. I don't think she has ever noticed a bacon slicer in her life, which is odd, because big shiny slicers used to be a focal point of grocery shops—we still have a beauty in our shop.

I then piped up and said, "Don't be such morons, it's a Wimshurst machine. It generates electricity."

Grinny looked uneasy. I added, "The voltages are very high—thousands of volts."

Grinny looked still worse.

I said, "Wind her up and see if we can't get a spark or something."

Grinny said, "Please, children, I would prefer that you took that machine elsewhere."

We pretended not to hear and wound away like mad. Soon we had long snaky sparks going and Grinny was trying to look blank. The sparks were reflecting in the woodwork; the whole corner of the room was flickering blue.

As arranged, Mac said, "There must be some power behind all that! I mean, just look at the sparks!"

I said, "Nonsense, no power, just volts."

He said, "Well, I bet you wouldn't put your hand through the spark!"

I pretended to be half afraid but boastful. In the end, after a lot of "I will!" and "You won't," I did put my hand in the spark and got the tickling I expected. I then made a great song and dance about it—jumped up in "agony" but said, "Told you so, didn't hurt a bit, couldn't hurt a flea," etc.—and eventually made Mac and even Beth be as "brave" as I had been. Grinny was getting very uneasy all this time. I saw her put her hand to her face in an uncertain dabbing sort of way, get half up in the chair, open her mouth without saying anything, etc. She never changed color, however. She never does.

We pretended to become boisterous and overexcited. We pulled the machine around on the floor so it got closer to her, then lifted it onto a table in the middle of the room and started twirling the handle again. Then we began whispering and at last Beth said, "I bet she would! You would, wouldn't you, Grinny?"

Grinny said, rather jerkily, "I would what?"

"Put your hand in the spark! It feels terrific! All tingly and funny!"

Grinny said, "Certainly not, no, no. Certainly not."

But Beth was well into her enthusiastic TV Kiddie routine and was saying, "Oh, but it's marvelous, it's fantastic, we all did it. Oh, be a sport, I told them you would!" And Mac and I lifted the machine off the table and brought it to a table next to Grinny's chair. She stood up and made a sort of noise but Mac pretended not to notice and wound the handle to make the sparks come and Grinny backed away and fell back in her chair again.

At this moment, Father came in.

What happened next is obvious enough without being written out in full. The words Fresh, Brat, Pest, Bloody Impertinence, etc., etc., resounded freely through the ancestral halls. Mum came in. She sized up the situation in an instant by forcefully mentioning the word teasing, which is precisely what we had been doing. We had been teasing Grinny in an attempt to get an indicative response.

When Mum had quite finished with us (Father standing behind her, jetting in the occasional expletives) we were feeling not only thwarted—for we had never finished our experiment—but also humiliated. It was Grinny who came to the rescue.

She said, "I don't think they were teasing so much as testing! Don't you think that possible, my dear! An old lady like me. . . . No, I'm sure they meant no harm. And no harm is done, none at all."

"There are a few tests I can think of myself," said Father. "How strong is a walking stick? How flexible is a slipper? How sensitive is a backside?" This sort of talk means that he is beginning to enjoy a situation: it is when he is too enraged to do anything but utter monosyllables that you run risk of lasting physical damage.

Beth now rounded things off neatly and with excruciating bad taste by saying, in effect, "Oh! We are truly repentant! And all too conscious of shortcomings! We are but little children weak, not born to any high degree, forgive us our trespasses and never again shall we stray from the path of rectitude," etc., etc., etc., ad nauseam. Not that she spoke these words; all she needs is her eyelashes and a voluntary compression of the tear glands. What she did say was something about us not teasing, just testing (weally and twuly) and if Grinny wanted to test us right back, that was only fair.

68

To our surprise, Grinny took this up. She said that would be fun, she would like to test us. Was there a game called Memory or something?

From then on, the evening became a sort of Mental Agility Olympic Games. We played that stupid game with a tray—someone goes out and loads the tray with mixed things, all listed, then the tray is brought in and everyone tries to remember as many things as possible. Father always wins at this.

Grinny won.

Next we played the card game in which the cards are put on the table any old way, face up—then turned face down—and each person tries to name, from memory, the card he chooses to pick up. If you're right you just keep going, and the person with most cards wins.

Grinny won.

When I write "Grinny won," I don't merely mean that she won. She decimated, obliterated, smashed us. Her performance was not merely outstanding but phenomenal. Her memory wasn't just retentive; it was Total Recall.

March 12

When you think back on it, those memory games we played—in fact everything that happened that evening—proved yet again that Beth was right. The trick with the electricity is no longer important; we expected her to be frightened, she was frightened, so that's that.

But the memory games are another matter. What I think happened is that she simply was not aware of her extraordinariness when she infallibly got the right card or remembered each and every item on the tray. To her, it was just normal practice, just as it is normal for a cat to leap from floor to mantelpiece and land up there without disturbing a single object. Humans can't jump five or six times their own height and land like a computer-programmed feather; very few humans could compete with Grinny when it comes to remembering things.

But now look at Grinny's contradictions! Here is a person who cannot remember chestnuts—but can remember every card in the pack.

You can go on like this forever—contradiction after contradiction in the things she *can* do and *can't* do.

Add all the rest of the extraordinary things about Grinny (including my parents' relationship with her—why do they never question her about leaving, about our grandmother, about anything?) and you come to this:

Beth is right—Grinny isn't real.
But you also come to another thing or two.
IF SHE IS NOT HUMAN, WHAT IS SHE?
WHY IS SHE HERE?
WHAT IS SHE FOR?

Diary

BOOK TWO

April 10

It's late at night and perhaps that has something to do with it. But I've been rereading my diaries, looking back to those days in late February and early March and thinking—well, what *have* I been thinking? "Stupid!" just about sums it up. Stupid, imagine being so nice-minded about Grinny. Stupid, imagine not seeing more clearly just how right Beth has been all along with her WAW sort of reasoning. Stupid, imagine sitting down and solemnly writing out all the things that make Grinny different from us—and still avoiding coming to the point, coming out with it by saying, "Grinny! You're a freak and I forgive you for that. But you're a dangerous freak. You're a threat, a menace, a *monster* with a capital M, like Movie Monster, Murdering Monster, Man-eating Monster."

No, it's worse than that. You're here for something. At the moment, you're just a sort of suitcase and nobody notices the ticking noise. Later—WHOOMPF!—and people screaming and bleeding, broken glass and blood on the pavement. "Oh yes, officer, I saw this feller with the suitcase sure enough, I saw him plain, so I did, but how was *I* to know . . . ?"

But I can't say that, I can't pretend anymore. I have seen Grinny plain. I've seen her for a long time. I've seen my own parents not see her, so to speak. I've listened to Beth, but not listened properly because she's just my kid sister. I've been going around pretending to myself that it's all perfectly OK, mustn't make a fuss, doncherknow, not British. Like that story Father tells about the war, during the blitz. When the raid started they could actually hear the bombers overhead, so they all went into the hotel shelter—the story happened in a London hotel. But even in the shelter they could hear the bombers overhead going VOOM-er, VOOM-er, VOOM-er, and then they heard bombs falling. Everyone in the shelter was very quiet. Then there was the most colossal bang and plaster fell. Then there was another bang, even worse, the lights went out, they could hear the building falling down above them. Still nobody said anything. At last an American woman's voice, thoroughly bad-tempered and disgusted, yelled out, "For chrissake, WHY DOESN'T SOMEBODY SCREAM?"

As Father says, it was funny at the time, but the really funny thing was that the woman was right. It's not natural not to react.

And it's the same with Grinny. It's not natural for us just to sit here and say, "Oh, isn't it strange, here's this sinister freak come to stay with us forever and ever, she lights up at night and seems to have something to do with unidentified flying objects, please pass the rolls." We've got to get at her, find out more, look for her weak spots, discover what she's all about.

Talking about rolls, that song keeps going through my

76

mind. I can't remember it properly. It's on an old record of Father's, and starts off something like

> *The king of the Cannibal Islands*
> *Invited me to tea.*
> *And there at the top of the menu*
> *Was ME!*

That's the position we're in here. At the top of the menu, waiting to be eaten. But whether we're going to be served boiled, fried, or just docile, I don't know. We must find out, we must.

I suppose I'm writing all this strong-arm stuff just to nerve myself for what's ahead. It's so still and cold and calm tonight. You look out into the garden and there it is, quite still and bleached by the moonlight. Nothing moves. Everything seems to be waiting, waiting, waiting. Waiting for what? For lights in the sky and a thundering noise and lots of little green men getting out of a spaceship, then walking up the garden, very fast and determined? I'd believe that, I'd believe anything at this moment. But there's nothing out there, nothing at all, not even a cat or two. Not a thing moves.

It's the same in my room, I mean, I'm here, I can move. I stood in front of the mirror a minute ago and made faces at myself. I winked one eye, then put out my tongue, then raised an imaginary hat to my reflection. They used to do a gag on that in the silent movies. You'd have the villain feeling very suspicious—he thinks he's being watched and of course he is; the chief comic, made up to look just like the villain, is in the room with him. So the villain goes up to an open space, a connecting door for instance. He takes it for a mirror. He starts going through all sorts of ridiculous motions. And the comic, pretending to be his reflection in the "mirror," imitates everything he does. It gets funnier and funnier because you're sure the comic can't keep it up. And in the end he doesn't, he makes a wrong move. It really is very funny, terrific.

And yet when I was doing it just now—making faces at my reflection—it didn't seem funny at all, just sort of *frozen* and *waiting*. The whole room feels like that. The whole house does. As if something were going to happen, not now, not just yet, but soon enough. The house has felt like that ever since Grinny came. No, that's not true— ever since Beth started her hate act. If Beth hadn't come out and said it, would anyone else have done so?

I wonder what Grinny's doing now? I wonder if she really does sleep in some way, like we do? Or is she just lying there on the bed, ticking away like my clock? It makes a terrific racket, no wonder I can't sleep. If you can't sleep, it's better to get up and do something, lying in bed listening to your heart beat doesn't do any good. So I got up and wrote in my diary. In the morning, of course, everything will be the same as ever—Mum yelling the time at me and sending Beth up to get me out of bed and Father losing things and the trees moving again in the garden.

But even in the morning, there'll still be Grinny.

We've got to do something about her or *to* her. It isn't just the night and the quietness. I've got this feeling that there isn't much time. We must think of something to *do*.

April 13

Tried "Eyes Right" on Grinny. It worked. Could it be the breakthrough. . . ?

April 14

We tried it again today—Eyes Right—and it worked just as well as before. It works on Grinny just the same way it works on anyone normal, only more so. I remember Mac and I once made Beth almost hysterical when we kept Eyes Right up for a whole afternoon. The effect on Grinny is even more dramatic: it doesn't just upset her, it seems to throw her right off her tracks. Even I would call the effect sinister.

The beauty of Eyes Right is that no outsider can really be positive you're doing it. So you cannot be accused of anything. Not that I would mind much if someone did accuse me. I am sick and tired of the whole Grinny situation and the sooner we can bring it out into the open the better. Beth was right all along. It only remains to find out just what she was right about.

Mac wanted to make what he called an Elegant Variation and do it to the left instead of the right, but I said no, we'll stick to Eyes Right. It must always be done the same way so that the effect builds up.

So after dinner, when we were alone with her, we gave her the treatment. We all stared at a point just one foot to the right of Grinny's head whenever we spoke to her, instead of looking her in the eye in the usual way.

We opened the proceedings by a minute or so of silent

Eyes Right. Then Beth said, "I did like the pudding, didn't you Grinny?"

As before, Grinny was shifting in her seat, trying to get into our line of sight. She was twitching toward the place where our eyes were all focused. She said, "I have a slight headache. I am not well tonight."

Mac said, "Can I get you an aspirin?" She tried to catch his eye, but couldn't, of course. She bobbed to the right and said, "Oh, no, it is nothing serious."

"Let me get you one," said I. She tried to focus me but couldn't.

Beth said, "Is it very bad, Grinny?" and Grinny was obliged to look at Beth . . . who was looking where Grinny wasn't. Anyhow, it went on and on until she started dabbing her hand toward her face as if trying to reassure herself that she was there.

Then the next stage set in. She began to lose her temper. She became waspish, just like the last time. She said something about "behaving oddly," which was a mistake—Beth got to her feet and went nearer Grinny, still looking one foot to the right of her eyes, and said, "Oh, Grinny, do let me get you an aspirin, you must have such a bad headache." Of course, the nearer you get to the person, the worse the effect is. Grinny started to twitch her mouth and shift her head. But as usual she never changed color. Nor did she breathe faster.

In the end, the same amazing thing happened as before.

She seemed to go into a funny state where she was only half with us. She started speaking in "Grinnish"—a very fast twittering sound, much faster than a real person could talk, all mixed up with ordinary English. Her eyes were not focusing, they were flittering about very slightly. I am going to try and write down what she said in this condition:

> *I do not know why they you impolite so very rude inconsiderate mean no harm* (Grinnish' for some seconds) *perfectly calm such charming children not at all could not possible guess* (Grinnish) *look here here* (very fast) *look at me me me the girl knows nothing everything* (Grinnish) *it was a mistake oh dear me quite a serious mistake a mistake but none of us is perfect not a vital mistake but a mistake* (Grinnish) *too late to remedy knowledge is power look at me* LOOK AT ME (Grinnish). . . .

These are not her exact words, they could not be. She was gabbling, sometimes very fast. She accelerated until she lapsed into the twittering of Grinnish, then came out of it back into our language.

The things I have got right, however, are important. The *feeling* is right, I am sure. She seemed to be practicing clichés, set phrases—"none of us is perfect" is obviously a phrase she had picked up and saved for future use in ordinary conversation.

It is important that she said, "Look at me, look at me." She must have had at least a suspicion of what we were doing to her with our Eyes Right trick—but she did not know the countermove; she didn't know how ordinary people would behave (Father, for instance, would just have said, "All right, joke over!").

There is another possibility, though. Perhaps she never

knew that we were playing a trick at all. Perhaps she thought that something was wrong with her own body—that it had slipped in space.

This could be the answer. I can easily imagine myself, wearing the skin and bones of an alien being, finding things just a little difficult now and then. You have been briefed on every possible thing—your bosses instruct you that you show you are pleased by bending up your mouth *so* . . . the word for that is "smile" . . . that when you sit down, your legs must not straddle apart if you are a lady . . . that you do not touch people or let them touch you very much—though sometimes a human may come up to you, take hold of *this* hand, the *right* hand, and shake it up and down. Or even press his or her food-hole against your face!—a kiss.

Right. Fine. You learn all these millions of crazy rules —you have a fantastic memory—but you still make mistakes. For instance, you *reveal* your fantastic memory, which is itself an error. You appear to believe impossibilities. And when the Eyes Right game is played on you, you know something is wrong, *but you don't know what!* You think, "It could be me, I've slipped sideways in my alien skeleton and skin!" Or you think, "This must be one of the things these foreigners sometimes do . . . I dare not make any comment." You could react in any of a dozen ways, all of them wrong.

I will write down what I think happens to Grinny when we give her the Eyes Right treatment. It is this:

She feels the same uneasiness, even fear, that humans feel—that a dog can feel. The fear turns to a sort of panic. Then the panic, in Grinny's case, turns to a hypnotic condition of some sort. She is not only feeling—literally—out of place: she also feels out of character, out of mind. Again literally, she does not know where she is.

And that is why she lapses into Grinnish—*which I assume to be her own language.*

And serve the old hag right. It's only justice. She says, *"You remember me"* to adult humans, and puts them into some sort of coma. We do an Eyes Right on her, and accidentally discover that we can do much the same thing to her—put her in a coma.

Serves her right.

April 18

Got Grinny in the garden, on her own. We maneuvered her nearer and nearer the swimming-pool motor to soften her up (fear of electricity), then started the Eyes Right, all three of us. It was faster this time, she tranced very quickly without much resistance. Strange feeling in open air watching "old lady" gibbering and squeaking, then talking polite old-lady English.

(Am writing this fast because something is going to happen, soon, and I want to leave a record—but everything is in a mess because of Mac's hand and the big fuss, so must scribble.)

Beth looking very mean and purse-mouthed, obviously determined to have a try but not knowing how. Grinny babbling. Mac accidentally started Grinny off by trying to get through the trance to her. He said, "Tell us about spaceships," or something but no reply, so he said, "You can tell me, Grinny, it's Mac, *you remember me*" (!!!)

This is Grinny's own trigger phrase, and it made a bang all right—she suddenly came right out of her trance, snap! and looked about her for a split second, then fastened on Mac and said, "I beg your pardon?"

Then she reached out her hand and took Mac's hand. He jerked. She seized it. He went white straight away, she must have hurt him. She looked at him with her mouth working but not saying anything, then at last she said,

"It is not polite. . . . It is not polite to . . . not polite."
While she was saying this, I saw Mac's hand go dead
white. The pressure from her horrible little steel claws.
He jerked. She let it go for an instant, but then grabbed
again and caught his thumb and he let out a yelp. She was
still trying to find something to say, she said, "Most upset,
cannot understand . . ." and Mac had tears coming out of
his eyes from the pain. I don't think she knew she was
putting on so much pressure. He made a sort of snatch
trying to get his thumb away but she snatched too and
there was a dull click and Mac screamed and went down
on his knees.

When she did let go, she looked puzzled and uncertain.
Beth went tearing in, hitting G. with fists and screaming
and screaming. Mac still on ground, doubled up white
as a sheet, clutching his hand and saying, "Bloody hell,
bloody hell."

Beth's yelling heard by Mum, who opened window and
shouted for Father. They came out running and everyone
was explaining things at the same time. Father made
everyone shut up, turned to Grinny for explanation. She
said something about the children teasing, but Beth tore
in again. Father lost temper and hauled her away calling
her a brat, etc., etc., if ever any of us behaved like this
again he'd chuck us out of house. (Mac ignored—nobody
knew his thumb was busted yet.)

Beth turned on Father and screeched, "Why don't you
throw her out? Why is she still here?" She turned to Mum
and asked the same thing—beseeching is the word. Beth
was begging them to get rid of Grinny, but of course they
had the old block, the hypnosis or whatever it is; they

cannot answer such questions, Grinny has got their minds tied up.

All quiet now, ha ha, that's a laugh, all quietly murderous. Mac has been driven to doctor, then home, thumb busted. Beth with me. Like a caged tigress. Wants to kill Grinny, then parents, then anyone handy. Grinny not giving a damn either way because Father and Mum cannot be reached by us about anything concerning Grinny. No doubt she's doing crossword and looking sweet.

After all that twittering I wonder if—

April 19

Yesterday's entry ended "I wonder if . . ." Then I had to go downstairs to be bawled at by Father, who is pathetically determined to be master in his own house, etc., etc. If only he knew! But it's not his fault, of course, so I just stood there and let it roll.

What was I wondering if? I was wondering if, after all the Grinnish twittering of yesterday, there would be some response from Out There, the Wild Blue Yonder. So I rang up poor Mac, who is in agony (I got my thumb yanked right back once and know how it hurts) and asked him—if he couldn't sleep during the night—to look out of the window now and then. He caught on at once, but said nothing would happen. I said it might, because things were so obviously coming to a climax and Grinny might need advice.

I set my alarm for two in the morning. I woke up when it rang, set it for three, and went to sleep again. I slept through it, though, but luckily woke up at ten to four and set the clock for four thirty. If I had woken up at three as planned and then set the clock for four I would have missed the whole thing. As it was, I could not have timed it better.

It was there all right. The sky was cloudy and sometimes you could only see a glow behind a cloud. But then the clouds scudded by and I saw it plainly, just the same as before. The same shape, the same lights, the same way of taking up a new position in a sudden, instant-acceleration rush. The same spacecraft as before.

I got out of bed quietly and quickly. I did not need anyone else, of course. Except that I was very frightened. I crept down the corridor and got to Grinny's room. When I looked through the keyhole I could see the glow. I started opening the door, turning the handle a bit at a time.

Just when I'd got the handle turned (but I was still outside the door) she woke up. Her lighting system dimmed and I heard the bed creak as she sat up. I could just imagine her doing it—straight up from the hips, as if she were hinged in the middle, like the last time.

The difference between the last time and this time was that this time I recognized the sound coming from her mouth even though I was nowhere near her. It wasn't my pulses zizzing and pumping, as I had thought the other time. It was her, Grinny, giving out with some Grinnish. She was twittering to the spacecraft and no doubt it was twittering back to her.

Then I heard something I had not expected at all—her voice speaking in plain English. An old lady's voice, a nice, well-bred old lady's voice, saying something very old-ladyish.

"Quite suitable," she said. "I see little difficulty. The sooner the better."

There was a brief pause. I heard some twittering, not Grinny's. It must have been the reply from the spacecraft, it was not at the same pitch as hers.

Then Grinny said, in a low, calm voice, "You may come in now, Timothy."

April 19 (continued)

I am doing this on my typewriter, as there is so much to write and typing is faster. I am taking several carbons and will think later on about where to send them, although I don't suppose it will do the least good.

Which is just what Grinny thinks. "You may come in now, Timothy" she said—so I went in. Or tottered in. I could not stop myself shaking. It was not like being frightened, it was more like going to some large and respectable person who you knew was about to tell you in a very correct voice that you were going to die in five weeks precisely, or be expelled from school for some disgusting crime which would be written up in the local papers.

She switched on the little light, settled back on her pillows, and said, "You can sit on the edge of my bed if you wish. Are you cold?"

I said, "No."

She said, "Neither am I. I do not suffer from heat or cold or toothache or any such things, as I think you know. Even if you break my wrist, I feel no pain. And it mends itself almost instantly, which is *most* convenient."

I said, "Mac feels pain. You broke his thumb."

She said, "You sound upset. If you like, you may break a finger of mine. For Mac."

She held out her old hand with the fingers spread. "*Any* finger," she said.

I made some sound or other and flinched back from her.

90

She said, "You are afraid, and quite rightly. It is quite correct that you should be afraid, quite in order. You must not mind, Timothy. You must get *used* to it, indeed you must. The strangeness of it all. . . . You must accustom yourself to it."

She still had her hand stretched out. Then she took hold of one of her fingers with her other hand and gave a sudden twist. The finger she broke just split open. The skin parted and it split open. The finger was twisted and it was all out of line with the other fingers. There were little metal bones inside the split skin and some of them stuck out, glinting.

I thought I was going to be sick and was floundering about rather. She soon put a stop to that, however. She said, "There! You must accustom yourself to it, it is a fact of life, Timothy. I am a new fact of all human life."

I was still trying to edge away but she grabbed my wrist with her hand—the one with the broken finger—and pulled me toward her. Her hand was like a steel vise with plastic jaws. Its power was awful and unbelievable. She twisted her hand and my wrist so that the broken finger was right in front of my face and I was staring at it.

"Tell me when you are used to it," she said.

I said, "All right, all right, I'm *used* to it," and she let me go. I wish my voice had sounded different.

"Better soon," she said, almost coyly, looking at her finger. I could not look.

"Poor Mac," she said. "That was an accident. You children were very naughty and I found your game most confusing. Looking at me like that. . . . Or rather, not looking at me. But there we are, boys will be boys. That is one of your sayings, is it not? It is, isn't it? You must speak when you are spoken to, Timothy."

I said, "Yes."

"Consider my position," she went on. "Think of the difficulties! Imprisoned in this ridiculous artificial body of mine. Even more ridiculous if it were real. . . . One must not think of oneself, your difficulties too are considerable. I would not like to be a human, Timothy, really I would not."

"I wouldn't like to be you," I said. I wanted to sound defiant but it came out wrong. Sullen.

"A new fact of all human life," she said. "This is what you have to face. Things are going to change, Timothy. Change soon, change a great deal. You must accustom yourself. You are young and therefore adaptable."

"What about my parents?"

"They will find a part to play when things have changed. But they will not be aware of the change, Timothy, that is the important difference. You will know. They will not. But I think you have guessed that."

"You got at—hypnotized—them. Why not us?"

"See if you can guess," she said. Again, her voice had that horrible flirty ring to it, the tone of voice you heard when respectable old ladies try to wheedle store clerks. Perhaps she did not mean her voice to sound that way, but it did and it made everything worse.

Anyhow, she asked me to guess the reason and I replied, "I suppose you thought that children were too stupid to do you any harm. To put up a fight."

She said, "Yes, that was among the reasons, Timothy. *Among* them. After all, it is very difficult for the young.

One hardly expects grown people to listen to the arguments of children, let alone allow children to influence grown-up policies and actions. . . ."

She left a long questioning pause and I felt I was supposed to say something. I said, "Well, what are the other reasons?"

She replied, "I think you have guessed them, for you are quite intelligent—no, very intelligent, far more intelligent than I would have supposed. Very intelligent."

I said, "Thank you kindly, ma'am," trying to be sarcastic. But of course this was above her head and she paid no attention to it.

"The most important reason," she went on, "is this. When one tries an experiment, one must have what you people might call a 'control'—that is, a thing unaffected by the conditions created by the experiment itself. For instance, Timothy, if I were to enter your classroom at school and say to the teacher, 'Carry on as usual, pay no attention to me, I am merely a visiting supervisor!' the mere fact of my presence would be enough to ensure that the teacher and the pupils could *not* carry on as usual."

"So if you hypnotized everyone, adults and children alike, you'd never know how humans really do behave?" I said. But I was thinking about something else.

"Quite so. We left the children alone. First, because we thought they could do nothing to obstruct us; and second because we had to have free, natural, unaltered actions and responses to observe."

"Responses to what?" I said. I was still not really listening. I was thinking hard.

"Oh, to anything, anything at all. Everything. After all,

a human being is a human being, whether it is aged six or sixty."

"So we are all the same, are we?" I said.

"Oh, certainly not!" she said. "That is one of the *many* things I have discovered that surprised me. You are *very* different from each other. Far more different than *we* are, in the place where I come from."

"So all your prying and peeking in the swimming pool wasn't wasted, then."

"Oh, how very sensitive you are about that!" She laughed. "It interested me greatly, your response to my prying and peeking. I looked up some words in a dictionary and tried to make a rhyme about human sex. 'Prudery, nudity, rudery, crudity . . .' "

"I am glad you find it all so funny," I said, trying to sound dignified.

"The *facts* are not very interesting or amusing," she said. "But human *reactions* to facts are always interesting. And sometimes very funny indeed. The thing that most puzzles me about you humans," she went on, "are the extraordinary contradictions you display. You are the most humorous race we have yet encountered—but the very things about which you make jokes are those that puzzle and distress you. To make your excellent jokes, you must have great insight and knowledge: yet having made the jokes, you remain as ignorant and insightless as ever."

"There is no such word as 'insightless'," I pointed out.

"Impercipient?" she said. "That could be the word. It was in the crossword puzzle of February the twelfth. How very difficult those puzzles are for a stranger!"

"But we're still a simple little lot?" I continued. "No trouble at all to super brains like yours?" I was still thinking, in the back of my mind, about how to murder her.

"All the trouble in the world!" she said. "I never realized, until I came here, how powerful *emotions* could be! Reason against emotion . . . any civilization must fight that battle. Your civilization is quite advanced, quite well developed. Yet despite your achievements, your emotions seem to dominate you! You have only two sexes and you make more fuss about them than we do about five. You invent excellent weapons with which to slaughter each other, then weep when a puppy dies. Really, Timothy . . . if only you could look at yourself—at the whole of your race—*without* emotion, I think you would agree with me that you are quite—quite—oh dear, what *is* the word?—"

"Suitable," I said, flatly.

Her manner changed. She stopped being a nice old lady.

"Yes," she said at last. "You are a very intelligent boy, Timothy. 'Suitable.' I wonder how many of my own sons —I have a great number, far too many—would have understood so much from a single word."

"It wasn't from a single word," I said. "It was from all kinds of things." I was going to say more—to mention her fear of electricity, her speaking "Grinnish," her worried look when we pretended we had been seeing UFO's for years—but shut myself up in time.

"But it all comes down to one word now, doesn't it?" I went on. "We're 'suitable' so it's game, set, and match."

"I beg your pardon?"

"You have won. And nothing can stop you."

"That is right. Timothy," she said. "Nothing can stop us."

She settled back in her bed and said, "Look, my finger is almost healed. You may go to bed now, Timothy. Good night."

I went to bed and thought. I thought about how to kill her. But then I thought, "What difference would it make?"

April 20

I see that I have failed to make myself clear in what I wrote yesterday, so this time I am going to put down all my conclusions in an orderly manner.

SITUATION

Our so-called Great Aunt Emma is an alien being from another planet, sent to find out how suitable this planet may be for invasion by her species. She is the advance lookout for an invasion. Her job is to evaluate and understand us—to find out how much opposition we would be likely to offer the invaders, how "suitable" we are. The thing has been tried before—but other places weren't "suitable." Our planet is.

METHOD

To enter our home, Grinny hypnotized all adults she met by using the phrase "You remember me." She used this phrase on adults only. She took the children as she found them because she thought that (a) children could not offer effective opposition and (b) because she needed to observe human beings in their natural, unhypnotized condition.

RESPONSES

The children soon discovered that there was something "wrong" with Grinny and tried to find out what was wrong by laying traps for her. While they were doing this, they felt they were making important and progressive discoveries. What they failed to realize was that Grinny did not very much care one way or the other. If the children had said, "There! We have found you out! You are an alien!" she could have replied, "Yes, quite right—and what are you going to do about it?"

POWERS

Any adult Grinny meets, she can control instantly. Presumably she could do the same with children if she wanted to (she nearly hypnotized me).

She can communicate with her superiors or allies or whatever they are—the beings in the spaceship. But she cannot do this at very long range. If she could, why should the spacecraft have to come within sight of our planet?

She has great physical strength in her nonhuman body but I do not think this important. Certainly not to her. Her body has been made to measure for the job of posing as a human being. When she has no further use for it, she will assume her own shape and body.

She seems to have great mental powers. Her memory is inhumanly good, for instance. But it does not seem that she has comic-strip, superhuman powers. For instance, she has to speak a language, and she cannot project thoughts or anything like that. She has to talk "Grinnish" to communicate with the spacecraft. Sometimes she says things that indicate that all is not well on her own planet. She told me that she has far too many children, for instance. I suppose you could say she is capable of being

98

indiscreet. But then, she is so sure of her powers and the powers of her race that she feels free to say anything she chooses.

I do not know what powers she and her race can bring to bear on us. If her race is capable of equipping Grinny with such a good "human" body, they can probably make anything they need in the way of weapons. We could never construct a Great Aunt Emma—a walking, talking, human-imitation, cigarette-smoking machine. They can. So presumably they've got the technology to invade us.

WEAKNESSES
Grinny has quite often made mistakes. She even has built-in mistakes—no human smell, skin cannot change color, many gaps in her programming or "education" about Earth things and ways. But as I have said, these mistakes cannot be of importance to her or her race.

PROBABILITIES
She told her contacts in the spacecraft that we are "suitable" (for invasion). She told me that we humans have got to come to terms with "new facts of human life"—in other words, with the things the invaders will do to us. She was not at all upset when I overheard this.

So presumably the invasion will come soon.

April 22

This evening the showdown came. She started it as much as we did, but we were perfectly willing for it to happen. It was about nine o'clock. The parents were watching the news on TV in the den and we were alone with Grinny. She sat in the big armchair and we were sitting around uneasily, waiting for things to start.

She said, "Well. Well, well, well. The time, the place, and the loved ones all together. Do you know, Timothy, I think one could conduct the whole range of human affairs solely at the level of quotations! What a wordy lot you humans are!"

"That was a misquotation," I said.

"Oh, I know, it should be 'loved one'—the singular, not the plural."

"What immortal hand or eye could frame thy fearful symmetry," said Mac. He had been doing Blake at school.

"That's very apt, Mac," Grinny said, "William Blake, isn't it? You are referring to monstrous old me, of course. Well, I cannot pretend to be symmetrical, but I admit to being rather fearful. And also fearless, quite fearless. For what have I to fear from you children?"

None of us could think of anything to say.

"We mustn't waste time, must we?" she said. "I'm

sure you are all bursting with questions—what is going to happen, when, where, what it will be like when it has happened. . . . Do feel free to ask anything you wish."

"Why don't you go away and leave us alone, you horrible old witch?" burst out Beth.

"A good beginning!" said Grinny. "Why won't we leave you alone? Because we need the space, my dear. Your space. And your amenities—your foods, minerals, water, lands, everything. Yours is by far the nicest planet we have seen. Ours is quite horrid—rather as yours will become not so many years from now, when you are all standing on each other's shoulders. But we will not permit that situation to arise, of course. You see, Beth, you have come to the end of your time; you humans have had a very long history, far too long. You have done too much, made too many mistakes—"

"While on your infinitely superior planet? . . ." Mac interrupted. He was twitching with anger.

"But it isn't infinitely superior," said Grinny. "As I say, it is quite horrid. Our problem is just the same as yours—overdevelopment and much too large a population. The difference is that we can do something about it and you cannot."

"When you invade us, what happens to us?" I asked.

"What happened to the peoples we invaded in the past?" said Grinny. "They went to the wall [what a strange expression! What wall?]. They served their new masters and were punished if they did not serve well enough. They were allowed to continue living if their lives were useful. The majority accepted their conquerors—as I hope you will. But those who caused trouble were pun-

101

ished or removed. I trust you children will not grow up to be troublemakers."

"We won't be allowed to be troublemakers," I said. "You'll hypnotize us all, or whatever it is."

"Certainly not!" exclaimed Grinny. She sounded quite shocked. "That would be folly! How could mere robots —people living in a trance—learn to serve us as we wish to be served? Oh, no, Timothy! The adults, yes, they will be hypnotized . . . just like your mother and father. They are past training, they hardly matter. It is merely a matter of keeping them quiet for a while. But you young people— by which I mean those that have not reached adolescence—you must be encouraged to expand and blossom and grow—"

"Into what?" said Mac.

"Into truly efficient servants! Servants with their own will and intelligence and ability to learn and even invent. But servants who can be formed in the necessary pattern, the pattern we require."

"It sounds lovely," said Mac, staring at her. "Just lovely."

"If you mean that—but of course you don't—you are greatly mistaken," said Grinny. "We will need a great number of things in a very short space of time if we are to survive on your planet. Our own resources will be quite inadequate. Even our machines will not be enough to build what we need. So it will be up to you humans for the first hundred years or so. Two generations, say. . . ."

"One and a half," Mac said rudely. "A human life is three score years and ten. That's a quotation."

Grinny looked at him for a moment or two and said, "A

human life will be two score years from now on. You may quote me."

I could see it all clearly enough. When the invaders came, we would be their slaves. Little children would be "educated" to serve. Older children would begin doing their work as soon as they were strong enough. An adult would work until he dropped at the age of forty or so. And if he didn't drop, he would be done away with. There would be no place for aging humans under the new order. No place for the sick, the weak, or the brainworkers. No place for my own mother and father.

Beth had not understood all this. She was looking from Grinny to me and Mac with wide, worried eyes. Her face was twisted with fear and hatred into an expression that came out as sheer spite.

She got up from the cushion on the floor where she had been sitting and said, "I'm going to bed. Good night, Mac. Good night, Tim."

She walked over to Grinny in the big chair and said, "Good night, dear Grinny-Granny."

Then she slapped Grinny as hard as she could, right in the face.

There was a complete silence until Mum spoke. We hadn't noticed her, she had been standing in the door with a cup of coffee in her hand. She had seen it all, of course.

Mum said, "Oh, are you off now, Beth? Well, good night, darling."

And Grinny looked at Mac and me with eyes that were expressionless before she said, "Good night, Beth dear. Sleep well."

April 23

We met in Mac's house because we wanted to get away from our own house and the feeling of Grinny being all around us.

"Meeting of the GCG called to order," said Mac. "Somebody start us off. . . ."

Beth made a vulgar noise and Mac said, "What's that for?"

"For being bloody silly," she replied, nastily.

"You shouldn't say 'bloody'! Girls shouldn't swear . . ." Mac began.,

"Bloody, bloody, bloody-blood BLOODY," Beth said. "The GCG . . . you make me sick!"

"I second that," I said. "It makes me sick too. We've had enough about GAE and GCG and Grinny-Granny. There's nothing for us to be funny about anymore, so let's talk seriously. Mac?"

"I want to start," said Beth.

"All right. Well?"

"I vote we kill her. Tonight."

"I suppose you're feeling bloody-minded enough," said Mac, emphasizing the "bloody" as a way of annoying Beth, "to do it yourself?"

"Yes," said Beth. She said the one word in a way that stopped anyone else from speaking. She sort of punched it at us. It made me feel sorry for Mac, feeling as he does about Beth. If he thinks she's some sort of fairy princess, that "yes" must have changed his mind.

"All right—how would you do it?" he said, rather feebly.

She said, "I'd get the big hammer and a poker and bash it through her head when she's asleep."

Mac said, "For heaven's sake!—"

"Or I'd push her against an electric fire, that radiant one, the one with the live wires," she continued. She did not speak at all loudly. Obviously she had been thinking about how to kill Grinny, and these were her answers. Mac and I couldn't think of anything to say. She suddenly noticed the silence and said, sounding like an ordinary little girl again, "It isn't as if she were human, is it?"

Mac started to say stupid things to her, calling her vicious and so on, until I cut in and said, "Beth's right. She's been right all along. Mac, you'd better shut up."

He said, miserably, "All right, then. What *are* we going to do?"

"First," I said, "we've got to make up our minds to it— Grinny isn't just some fairy-tale ogre, she's here and she's real and she means what she says. We've got to *win* against her. But that's not the same thing as killing her."

"Why not?" said Beth.

"Several reasons. Killing her proves to Them, whoever They are, that we've got a limited amount of power—but only limited. I mean, suppose Mac failed an exam at school, and he managed to get to the man who marked the papers, and attacked him. All right, the man's clutching his nose and saying 'Don't hit me again! You win!'—but it makes no difference, does it? Mac still hasn't passed the exam."

105

"I don't understand," said Beth.

"Tim means we've got to win a moral victory," said Mac. "But I don't suppose you understand what that means," he added bitterly.

"I do understand, I'm not stupid. Tim means it's no good just destroying her, that's not enough. But I'd like to do it just the same. Anyhow, there might be more of her."

"What was that?" I said. And Mac's mouth dropped open. "You mean, more Aunt Emmas? Ours isn't the only one?"

The idea stopped us cold. We hadn't thought of it before, I can't imagine why. Then Mac, having thought for some time, broke the silence. "No," he said. "I don't think so."

"Why?"

"Well, just think of the difficulties. I don't mean the production difficulties, you could just as easily make three of her as one, for all we know. But think of the risk! The risk for Them! Think what a chance they're taking planting just one Aunt Emma among us! I mean, we've already found out all about her, and we're not overbright. Suppose they picked someone stronger than us, or cleverer. Suppose, for instance, they planted an Aunt Emma in the right house but the wrong neighborhood—where there was some nervy and inquisitive character in the place who wouldn't let go—who'd keep probing and asking questions and—well, someone like Mrs. Thrupp."

We had a Mrs. Thrupp a few houses away and you couldn't stop her. Not only did she know all about everyone, she was quarrelsome with it. She liked picking fights about overhanging branches or children playing because in that way she could interfere with other people's business.

"Or suppose you'd listened to me earlier!" said Beth. Everything she says nowadays seems to have a nasty edge to it, but here again she was right. If Mac and I had been different people and Beth had been the same person, by this time we'd have done something about Grinny.

Mac said, "I don't think they'd take the risk of making more than one Grinny. And when she was showing off to us the other night, she didn't give the impression that she had any friends except Them, the spaceship bunch. Besides, there's still another thing."

"What?"

"It doesn't matter either way. It doesn't matter at all how many Grinnies there are. It's beside the point *as long as we don't kill her*. Killing her doesn't prove anything. Her masters would just write her off and say, 'All right, a pity, but we'll go ahead. Anyway, we don't need her anymore now!' No, what we've got to do is—make her surrender."

"Make her surrender!" Mac repeated. "That's it. She's got to tell them that we're not suitable. It won't do any good coming from anyone else."

"And once she's told them," I said, "it doesn't really matter if there are other Great-Aunt Emmas. As far as They are concerned, one single failure is enough. Just one voice saying 'Not suitable!' is all we need."

We were feeling quite pleased with ourselves at this point, having done our little logical exercises and come out correctly. But then Beth said, "All right. Now what?" and we were back at the beginning again.

We thought for some time and Mac said, "What about your parents? Couldn't we make an attempt to get through to them—to break through the hypnosis or whatever it is?"

Beth and I both said "No" at the same time. "I bet we couldn't, however hard we tried," Beth said. "And anyhow, it would take too long. I mean, even if we broke through, we'd still have to *explain*. It would take weeks."

"We've probably *got* weeks," Mac pointed out.

"No, we haven't," Beth said sharply.

"Why not? How do you know?"

"Because I know. And because she's told us so much. Something's going to happen soon; I know it is."

Neither Mac nor I felt like arguing this point.

"Well, what *can* we do?" said Beth.

"What weapons have we got?" said Mac.

"Only one," I said. "The only thing we've ever pulled on Grinny is the Eyes Right trick. I think she still doesn't really understand it. I mean, she knows what it is, and what's been done to her—"

"—But she doesn't know how *much* has been done!" said Mac. He was getting excited. "She talked about Eyes Right too calmly! It's like those people who are hypnotized on a show and made to do ridiculous things—you know, pretend they're monkeys and scratch themselves, that sort of thing—and when they come out of it, they just look around modestly and smile politely. Even when they're told what stupid things they did, they still can't believe—"

"It's the only thing we've got," I said.

"It's not good enough! I wish we could kill her, I wish we could do something to her!" Beth shouted.

I said, "Shut up, Beth. Unless someone can come up with something better, a new idea, we'll take a vote. Let's all sit still and think for three minutes by my watch. Beginning now."

I looked at my watch and we started thinking. At least, Mac and Beth probably did, but I couldn't. I was thinking of Beth and wondering if she was really such a blood-thirsty horror as she seemed, or whether it was just Grinny acting on her instinctively female responses—to put it less grandly, her built-in bitchiness. Just once, I'd seen my own mother turn into a screaming tearing wildcat. It was when a couple of teen-age bullies got hold of Beth behind the big tree in the playground. They didn't do anything much but when Mum caught them a day or two later in the village street, she just screeched and smashed and flailed. No man could have acted like that, let alone sounded like it. You'd have thought she was mad, but she was right. I thought Beth mad, but she'd been right.

Before the three minutes were up, Mac said, "It's obvious. Eyes Right, emotions, electricity. They're our weapons. Any argument?"

"No," I said.

"No, but soon," said Beth. "Tonight."

We talked some more, deciding just what to do, then broke up.

"Tonight, remember," said Beth. "Not later."

April 24

Grinny again in the big chair, holding court. Telling us about the new order. Another installment of the same nightmare.

We gave her the Eyes Right treatment.

She said, "Yes, well, this is very amusing but rather naughty of you. I have endured a lot of teasing from you children, all kinds of mischief and tricks. I don't know if it has occurred to you that I have one or two tricks of my own."

She pulled something out of her handbag. It looked like a large, smooth pocket flashlight. She held it in her hand.

I think it was this flashlight thing that started Beth off. We had agreed to push emotions at Grinny as hard as we could go, as well as giving her the Eyes Right. We had even agreed, in a silly sort of way, what emotions each of us would try to project (Beth simply said, "Hate!"). The trouble was that, apart from Beth, we were beyond emotion. Mac and I agreed that we both felt merely—sick. Sick with fear, sick with worry, sick with tiredness (neither of us could sleep properly and when we did sleep we had dreams). Perhaps it would have been different if we had known just when the thing was going to happen —just when the spaceship would land, just what the invaders would look like. But we knew nothing and Grinny wouldn't tell.

All we knew was that sooner or later, it would happen. Adults over here, children over there. Get marching. If you didn't march, something to tickle you up and make you. No time for good-byes—no reason for them, even. The parents would talk about all the usual home affairs—Marjorie's grades, how expensive good beef is, let's have coffee at eleven on Tuesday. . . . And some of the little children would shriek and cry and tug at their mothers' skirts, but mother would just turn around and say, "Oh, you are being naughty today—run and join the other children over there like a good girl. Mummy will be with you in just one moment." And there they would be, the hypnotized and the unhypnotized, the grown-ups chattering away politely as they were herded away together to be wiped out and the children, alone, screaming and yelling and begging in an agony of fear as the world came to an end.

At least, that is how it is in one of my dreams. There are several variations, some of them highly spectacular and bloody. It is just the same for Mac, of course.

Meanwhile, we go to school and do our homework and eat our dinners and lie awake in bed. When you have done this for a week or so, emotions are hard to come by. You just feel sick and rotten and hopeless.

Anyhow, Grinny pulled out the flashlight thing and Beth tautened like a cat. But she must have still kept on with the Eyes Right. I know I did. I suppose the emotion I put out was fear and anger. The same for Mac. But with Beth it was spitting, violent, killing hate.

It reached Grinny. She went under.

"I have one or two tricks of my own," she had said.

Immediately Beth got to her, Grinny's voice changed. "Useless!" she grated (she really did grate the word out, right from her throat: you can hear it on the tape, I had the recorder running). "Useless—how dare you—most certainly not. . . . Will not permit . . . most severe and painful punishment . . . painful, terribly. . . . I warn you, here in my hand. . . ."

She lapsed into Grinnish. The flashlight thing had fallen into her lap, but her hand was still clenched as if she were holding it. We kept up the Eyes Right pressure and I heard Beth muttering. She was saying, "I *hate* you, I *hate* you, I *hate* you. I want you to *die* and *die* and *die*."

Then Grinny was talking again. She said, "A temporary embarrassment. Bring them to order, to heel, discipline . . . in good time, merely temporary difficulty . . . once we are overwhelming superiority will change and subdue, all in charge no further trouble, could not possibly allow . . . (Grinnish) . . . very powerful she is for such a small animal, oh how very powerful she is for such a small animal oh how powerful, oh how uncomfortable it is but still one must endure, merely a temporary situation. . . ."

She was talking of Beth and I think Beth knew what was happening. Beth was leaning right forward, glaring at a space one foot to the right of Grinny's eyes, mouthing at her. I glimpsed this out of the corner of my eye—but I could have felt it without seeing it, almost, her hatred was so intense. A solid stream blasting from her mind into Grinny.

I tried to stop my brain from just watching and concentrate instead on projecting emotion at Grinny. I would go back to projecting Muddle. This is as close as I can get to naming my emotion. Confusion, muddle, worry, doubt, all made into a mixture to confuse and weaken Grinny. I suppose I was mouthing away too, saying things like, "You're wrong, you're failing, you're losing, you're done for, you're frightened!"

Mac had chosen Determination (he is very determined anyway). He was simply getting across the thought, "You won't, we will. You'll lose, we'll win. We're strong, you're weak."

Grinny was deep into Grinnish for quite a long time. She must have been greatly weakened. Her eyes were wide open, as if she were in a trance. Her mouth was open too. Her fingers were twisted and knotted in shapes I can't imagine in human hands. They were *writhing*.

I thought it a good time to go and get the camera. Part of the plan was to get together as much evidence as possible of the behavior and nature of Grinny in case we were ever lucky enough to reach some adult who would listen to us and be convinced and even take action.

So, still Eyes Righting, I got to my feet and slowly went to the door. The camera was there, fixed up with the electronic flash gear. I came back step by step, being careful not to step across the sightlines of Mac and Beth. I knew the camera was already correctly set for speed and opening.

I was afraid that the flash would spoil everything, but had to risk it. I took one of Grinny from about six feet, when her hands got into an extraordinary position and her dry open mouth was gaping at me through the viewfinder. The flash went off and she stopped speaking Grinnish immediately.

But she didn't come right out of her trance as I had feared, she just started talking English again. She said, "Special circumstances . . . not likely to be encountered when we have established our general, over-all superiority and ascendancy. Admittedly most uncomfortable, most, most, most, most . . . thrice blessed is he who gets his blow in first, a quotation."

I felt something touch my leg. It was Mac's finger. He was leaning forward, still Eyes Righting Grinny, but he wanted my attention. He flicked his eyes toward the French windows for a split second. I looked out of the window.

The spaceship was in the sky, closer than I had ever seen it before. So close that you could guess its height, only a few thousand feet. Its shape was crisscrossed by the branches of the lime tree in our garden.

I was shaken badly. Mac was too, for he began to talk his emotions. He began muttering, "We're *not* suitable, *not* suitable." He was doing this to make himself concentrate.

Grinny changed position in her chair like someone uneasily asleep. Her hands began to writhe again and I thought of photographing them because they were so strange and inhuman but I was afraid she might wake up. Then I thought (it wasn't easy to think and at the same time keep up the Emotion and Eyes Right) I should photograph the flashlight thing, which might be valuable evidence. I couldn't look at it myself, as I had to concentrate on Eyes Right. The spacecraft was still there, I could see it without looking at it as something bright at the edge of my vision. Mac was getting confused too by everything that was going on at the same time. Only Beth was really keeping going.

I suppose it was our weakening that made a change in Grinny. She began talking again, this time much more clearly and with expression in her voice. She said, "Most severe and painful discipline unless. I have only to give the order and the flashlight thing the flashlight thing you called it the flashlight thing will punish most severe and painful. Your silly tricks. I saw a flash, a flash of light. Your silly tricks."

But the flashlight thing was no longer there! It had disappeared—gone—vanished.

Beth was saying, "Die, die, *die!*" Mac said, "No, you won't, no, you won't; we are *not* suitable, *not* suitable!" And I was saying (or thinking, or both) the same thing as Mac—"*not* suitable, *not* suitable!" It was the reappearance of the spacecraft that had brought this phrase back, of course.

Then Mac changed his tune. He began to tell Grinny that the "flashlight thing" was no good, useless, she couldn't use it, couldn't touch it, couldn't reach it, etc. I thought this was a good idea of his. It turned out not to be.

Grinny suddenly woke some more. She said, "Emotion! Emotion! The mind!" Then she looked around her, just as people do when they wake up, and said, "You children are behaving very stupidly. I shall punish you if you continue, with the flashlight thing."

Mac then said, "You can't! It's gone!" and Beth screamed, "Gone! It's gone!" and started screeching with laughter. She was getting hysterical.

Grinny said, "Don't be so absurd, of course it has not gone!" She spoke as if she were not quite with the situation.

Mac said, "It's gone. It's out of reach, so it's no good to you."

Grinny looked surprised and puzzled and replied, "But you stupid child, *I do not have to touch it, it is worked by the mind!*"

There was a sort of gulf or vacuum for a second or two while the same thought hit all three of us: somewhere, Grinny's punishment machine was crawling around the room waiting for her instruction. When she gave it—when she flicked it on with her mind!—

I yelled, "Eyes Right!"

We all glared until our eyes were bursting and it worked. She shrank down again in her big chair and said, "Triggered by the mind, the mind." She was quiet for a moment. Then she said, very sharply and clearly, "Oh dear! I should not have said that! If the nasty children should hear. . . !"

But we *had* heard.

At last, Beth's voice said, hoarsely and softly, "Punish her."

We stared at the space one foot to the right of Grinny's eyes. Only Mac and I were in the right position to see the dull glint that appeared under the skirt of the sofa. The flashlight thing! The glint moved, slid across the carpet like a small rat and silently went toward Grinny.

Beth saw it and I heard her gasp. Then she said, "Punish her!"

Grinny said, "Most certainly not, most certainly. . . ! I

forbid. I am the master and you will obey me. . . ."

The glinting rat stopped.

I hissed, "Emotions!" We all clutched our minds together and beamed them at Grinny.

The flashlight thing slid onward toward Grinny.

"More!" I said. We gritted our teeth and poured the stuff at her. The flashlight thing slid smoothly up the side of Grinny's chair. She was wrestling with herself now, jumping and jerking in her chair. Streams of Grinnish came from her lips.

The flashlight thing paused—swayed—then dived into the sleeve of her dress. It went up her arm. It made a rippling hump under the fabric, all the way up her arm.

She made a horrible noise, a horrible noise, not a scream at all, it was like machinery tearing itself to pieces, like metal cutting metal. It went on and on and on until we couldn't stand it. She was flailing and whipping about with her arms in the chair.

I screamed out, "Stop it!—stop it!" and everything stopped.

She was still again. Her chair is the wing chair. One of the wings was broken and the cloth on the arms of the chair had been beaten through by her arms. Her sleeves were split and torn. So was the skin on her arms, it was torn. The metal bones showed through.

Yet her face was just the same as ever. The slight grin was still playing around her mouth. Her eyes were steady, her skin was neither pale nor red.

She said, "Please. Don't do it again. Please don't do it again. You know how afraid I am of electricity."

Mac said, "Electricity?"

"Blood," she said. "Some humans are afraid of blood, are they not? The life fluid. I am like them . . . afraid of the life fluid. . . ."

Her voice sounded so ordinary and old-ladyish and unstrained.

"You would not be so cruel!" she said. Then she repeated it, giving her voice human stresses and emotions. "You would not be so cruel!"

Mac said, "What do you mean, electricity?"

I said, "The flashlight thing punished her with electricity and she's afraid of electricity like some people—human people—are afraid of blood. Electricity is their life fluid, just like blood. Is that right?"

She said, "Yes. Please, *please* don't do it again."

Mac said, "You admit that we win?"

Grinny replied, "Yes, yes, anything you like. Just don't do it again."

"You admit our minds—our emotions—beat yours?" I said.

"Oh yes, yes." She was grinning politely.

Beth said, "I hate her! Don't trust her!"

I started to remove the flash head from the electronic flash. When you do this you expose a three-pin socket. You can put a variety of flash leads into the body. I took the extension lead and threw it to Mac. He always carries a penknife. I said, "Strip off the ends, Mac."

He began to bare the wires. Grinny said, "What are you doing?"

"We're not suitable, Grinny," I told her. "Not suitable at all. We are not going to be invaded."

"No, of course not!" she said. "What are you doing?"

118

"Do you know what Grinnish is, Grinny?"

"No. What are you doing?"

"Grinnish is the language you speak when you talk to the thing out there." I pointed out of the French windows. The spacecraft was no longer visible, but that made no difference. She knew what I meant.

"You're going to speak Grinnish, Aunt Emma. Now. You are going to tell your people that we're not suitable. Now or ever."

She began to knot her fingers and shift in her chair.

Mac said, "Catch." He threw the lead to me. I pushed the plug in. The three wires coming from it had shiny, raw ends. I opened my hand and held it, palm out, toward Grinny. Then I put the three raw ends in my palm and closed my fingers over them.

"If I pressed the button now, I'd get a shock," I told her. "Lot of volts. I don't know how much voltage that thing puts out"—I pointed to the flashlight thing—"but I'll bet this compares quite well. And it isn't controlled by the mind, it's controlled by a little red button." I showed her the button.

She said, "No. Please!"

"So if I put these wires in your hand, Grinny," I went on, "and if I tell Mac to press the red button, you'll get a shock of electricity. And there is nothing you can do to stop it. If you try to hypnotize us, you'll be too slow. If you get the flashlight thing going, you'll be too slow. If you blow the whole world up, you'll be too slow. Mac will still press the red button."

She said, "You mustn't, you mustn't."

"Say something in Grinnish, Aunt Emma," I said.

119

"I can't. I can't think of anything."

"Say 'the rain in Spain stays mainly in the plain.' It's a quotation."

"I can't. There is no word for 'Spain'—"

I went over to her and said, "Give me your hand." She held it out. I looped the wires over her middle fingers and twisted them tight. "Say it," I told her. "And when you come to 'Spain', say that in English." I caught Mac's eye and nodded toward the tape recorder. He went over to it. She looked at me with her emotionless eyes and said, "All right."

Then there was a split-second burst of Grinnish.

"Again."

Another burst.

"Again."

A third burst.

"Play it back on the slowest speed, Mac."

He played it back. Even on the slow speed, it was impossible to catch the syllables. But one thing was certain. The three bursts of sound were identical; and in each, there was the spitting sound that could have meant "Spain."

"We're not suitable!" said Beth. "Make her say that! Make her! Make her say it!"

"But I cannot possibly say it!" said Grinny. Her voice was loud and passionate. She must have concentrated hard to get so much human feeling into it. "They will be angry, very angry. . . ."

"Make her!" said Beth. She jumped up and gave the wire a little tug so that Grinny's finger jerked. "*Make* her!"

I said to Grinny, "You'd better tell them."

She said, "But I can't, I dare not."

"Tell them we are not suitable. Tell them we have weapons they can't defend themselves against. Tell them our planet won't be invaded."

"They will punish me—"

"Do it."

She spoke Grinnish for perhaps a second.

"Again. Tell them again."

She talked Grinnish again. Then she said, "Please take the wire off my finger. I have told them, I really have."

"How am I to know that?"

"I could make the spacecrafts appear again. That would prove I have been talking to them."

"Give them the message for the third time and make the spacecraft appear as well. But only for a short time. Make it appear for three seconds."

"Then will you take the wire off?"

I said yes, and she said words in Grinnish.

Almost at once, the spacecraft appeared. Mac and Beth ran to the window to look at it, but I stayed with Grinny and said, "I want to ask you questions about your planet and what you were planning to do to us. And about the flashlight thing—"

She said, "Oh! I forgot it! Oh!" She leaped to her feet and clumsily ran around the room, searching for the flashlight thing. She kept saying, "Oh! Oh!" in a metallic squawk. It almost sounded like an electronic signal, not a human cry of fear. But then she said, in a human voice, "I can't *think!* How can I control it if I can't *think?*"

I understood what she meant. She meant that she had no control over the flashlight thing; her mind was too hysterical to give it orders.

She stopped darting around for a moment to grip me with her terrible little steel hand and said, "You children! Think at it, stop it! Stop it, you must stop it, they will turn it on me!"

But even as she spoke, I saw the flashlight thing. It was behind her. It slid quickly across the carpet, then leaped at her hand. I saw it on her hand like a big metal leech— but only for a split second, for she started running, staggering, blundering around the room. She crashed into the standing lamp and it went down. There was a flash from the socket as something fused and the room was suddenly almost dark.

Then she was on the floor and there was the metal-cutting noise again and her screams, but they stopped just as they were becoming unbearable. I couldn't see much of what was happening and what I could see I could hardly believe. She seemed to be tearing herself to pieces; you could see fragments of cloth and patches of her skin and the glinting metal of her bones. There was a sort of drumming noise. It was her heels and elbows banging on the floor.

Beth was screaming, "I don't care, I'm glad" and sobbing and shuddering. Her eyes were completely round, she was staring at Grinny on the floor, still hating her. I thought she shouldn't be watching and put my arm round her, trying to push her head into my chest so that she couldn't see, but she just clawed my arm aside and went on looking. Mac was trying to get the lights to work. I am glad he failed.

And then all the noise and flailing motion stopped. There was just a small dragging, scraping sound. It was one of her arms. It was separated from her body. It was being pulled toward the French windows by the flashlight thing.

It went on like this, on and on. We three just stood there, cold with horror, while she was dismembered. The limbs and bits of machinery weren't so bad—it was the clothing that made you feel sick. Old lady's clothes, human clothes, with some busy, vile, alien machine inside them making them heave and twitch and bulge as it cut and ripped. The flashlight thing was as busy and unstoppable as a rat, never pausing from its nibblings and humped-up scurryings and lunges and tugs.

At last it had finished. What had been Great-Aunt Emma was a pile of garbage outside the French windows (it was Mac who opened them—I'd never have found the courage to get so near the horrors on the floor). Only one thing remained, gleaming on the carpet—a beautiful and elaborate metallic latticework cage about the size of a football, trailing filaments of metal thread like gold and silver hairs—spider-web hairs, like gossamer. No wonder she had been so frightened of our coarse electricity.

The flashlight thing arched its back and attacked the cage. There were sharp little clicks as the latticework was snapped or bitten through. A hole was made. The humped thing's back heaved and tugged industriously and something was pulled out through the hole.

It was another flashlight thing.

The two things seized the remains of the cage and hustled them to the pile outside.

They did not come back. The sky lit up and the spacecraft came closer than it had ever done before. I suppose the craft picked up the two flashlight things.

And I suppose one of them was Great-Aunt Emma.